The Bernardini Terrace

A JOAN KAHN BOOK

BOOKS BY SUZANNE PROU

The Bernardini Terrace

BY
SUZANNE PROU

TRANSLATED FROM THE FRENCH
BY ADRIENNE FOULKE

HARPER & ROW, PUBLISHERS
NEW YORK, EVANSTON, SAN FRANCISCO, LONDON

THE BERNARDINI TERRACE. English translation copyright © 1976 by Harper & Row, Publishers, Inc. All rights reserved. Printed in the United States of America. No part of this book may be used or reproduced in any manner whatsoever without written permission except in the case of brief quotations embodied in critical articles and reviews: For information address Harper & Row, Publishers, Inc., 10 East 53rd Street, New York, N.Y. 10022. Published simultaneously in Canada by Fitzhenry & Whiteside Limited, Toronto.

FIRST EDITION

Designed by Gloria Adelson

Library of Congress Cataloging in Publication Data

Prou, Suzanne.
   The Bernardini terrace.
   Translation of La terrasse des Bernardini.
   I. Title.
PZ4.P968Be5 [PQ2676.R64]   843'.9'14   75–25096
ISBN 0–06–013445–3

76 77 78 79 10 9 8 7 6 5 4 3 2 1

The Bernardini Terrace

THE TERRACE is long and narrow. To lay the dust and freshen the air, it is hosed down at sunset. The porous floor of octagon-shaped, precisely placed flagstones absorbs the water quickly and takes on soft hues of mauve, carmine, or ecru-yellow. When one walks on it in the twilight, one would think one were treading on a cloud of petals.

The plump posts that form the balustrade are reminiscent of period vases. In an unbroken file, they march the length of the terrace, and are doubled by a row of earthenware pots in which geraniums, hydrangeas, and fuchsias bloom.

The heightened scent of syringa mingles with the smell of damp stone.

One dreams of a balcony in Spain, or the inner court of an Oriental dwelling where rampant plants shed their leaves over a round fountain, or of a stone museum with windows that open onto a small public park.

It is the terrace of the Bernardinis.

Wedged between the arms of wicker chairs, with their feet propped up on stools, the old women talk: about the weather, the season of the year, the trifling events of the day, a death, a marriage. . . . Sometimes, in a slow, inward-sounding voice, they evoke memories, drop by drop. A silence follows, hollow and spherical, like a bubble in which they are suddenly enclosed. The beribboned phantoms of their youth flutter and brush against its smooth walls.

Tenuous scratchings, creakings, whisperings . . . Nothing happens, nothing will happen; time passes intact, for everything has already come to pass, and they face one further adventure only—their death. They are very old. Slowed to a standstill, as if mired in sand, they live a meager life. They draw their sustenance from their inexhaustible—and sometimes deceptive—memory.

The moment the lamp is lighted, moths arrive to beat against its enameled collar; they cast big shadows that dance over the old women's knees.

At one end of the terrace, the little door with its rounded top looks greener, and its diamond-shaped pane, carved from the evening dark, resembles an appliqué of black velvet.

Ensconced in the tallest chair, Mme. Laure Bernardini reigns in majesty.

Mme. Thérèse serves as lady-in-waiting, handing Madame her handkerchief or her fan.

The visiting Cygne ladies are twins—there is a strong resemblance—whose features and blue eyes must once upon a time have been much admired. Slowly they nod parallel profiles and shake their white curls.

Mlle. du Fleuriel is never without her silver-headed cane, which sometimes slips and scrapes against the wicker of her chair.

Mme. Constantin sucks on pastilles.

A distant clock strikes the hour. Mlle. du Fleuriel punctuates the strokes with her cane. When the last one sounds, she stands up; this is the signal for departure. The callers move in procession toward the door. They exchange two or three more remarks, the kind of thing one says in taking leave: "Another lovely evening . . . I hope you have a comfortable night. . . ." "Tomorrow the weather will be fine.

. . . The moon is clear. . . ." They disappear into the night.

Mme. Laure Bernardini goes into the house, followed by Mme. Thérèse, who carries her footstool and her shawl.

And Théo comes to turn the key in the lock.

I KNOW them well. Occasionally, accompanying my mother, I have slipped in among that covey of chattering old crows.

Or, rather, I think I know them.

I try to imagine that they were once young and beautiful, that they have had if not adventures, then at least a past. I should like to know why Mme. Thérèse sometimes permits a cruel gleam to filter between her eyelids, and why Mme. Laure, looking at Mme. Thérèse, often presses her violet lips together.

My mother is scarcely loquacious when I question her about her elderly friends. The past that she doles out to me in snippets does not suffice to weave the web of several lives. I am obliged to stitch bits and pieces together, to fill in gaps, the way one mends a worn counterpane with wool and odds and ends of chiffon.

It has become my game of patience. The people who surround me seem suddenly too young, too transparent. They lack the denseness, the mystery that I take pleasure imagining in the long, long past of these ladies in their black dresses. They fascinate me. Perhaps it is because they are standing on the threshold of death. Perhaps it is because they prefigure the ineluctable fate of each of us. They are the dark pool that sends back to us the image of our own future. They are also chests enclosing relics, opaque stones whose successive layers of sediment cover and imprison buried spangles—of gold, silver, or brass?

They have been; they scarcely are any more; tomorrow they will no longer be.

At the far frontier of their existence, I should like to detain them, open them the way one opens a coffer, read a kind of message that is about to be lost forever.

I stare at them. I grow drunk on their scent—orris powder and stale skirts.

Then I ask questions, and I collect a few images: some memories, some so-it-is-saids, some it-may-have-beens. . . .

I feel as if I were leafing through an album of old photographs inserted at random and, more often than not, lacking captions.

I classify, I imagine, I reconstruct. And figures rise from the bottom of time and begin to live again.

MME. BERNARDINI comes, people say, from a family of modest shopkeepers: butchers. It is hard to imagine her playing among slabs of raw meat or leaving tiny footprints in sawdust stained by the blood dripping from quarters of beef. Truthfully, one can scarcely believe that this elderly lady with the velvet-smooth cheeks was ever a child.

It seems, according to the town gossips, that the parents of Mme. Laure were ambitious. They were bent on keeping their daughter out of the shop from her earliest years, and they gave her what to them seemed "an education fit for a queen." One may assume, then, that she went into the butcher shop only rarely.

One visualizes young Laure installed on the second floor, in the room with the balcony that extended over the bright-red shop sign. Like Angélique in *The Dream*, seated by the window, some fancywork in hand, she occupied herself with a piece of delicate embroidery, now and then glancing down into the street at the good housewives bustling back and forth across the square.

Did she like her solitude, her proper young lady's tranquility? Did she take pleasure in the fact that she lived a floor above her parents, while they busied themselves below, smiling at customers and rolling roasts between their hands?

She would look pensively at her own slender white fingers; she would take a stitch, then another; she would lift her gold thimble in the light.

She was a little bored but accepted her boredom as an unavoidable penalty, the price that had to be paid for her to become "somebody," just as her father and mother accepted their promiscuity with escalopes of veal.

She did not even prepare their meals; the maid saw to that. At noon, she would watch her parents arrive breathless, happy to see her, bearing the cash from their morning's work in an old brown leather pouch.

They called her "little girl" and "doll." And it was true that she looked like a doll: straight-backed, pretty, stiff, with porcelain-blue eyes and a narrow-pleated linen blouse. Was she blond or brunette? Her mother surely put her hair up in paper curlers and, in the morning, rolled the curls on a round stick.

There was a café directly opposite the shop. How else would she have been able to observe, through the light curtains at her window, the town's fashionable young people who made her heart beat faster? She knew that the reward for her parents' labor and her own endless wait would be her marriage, her fine marriage. Just as she forbade herself to talk shop, leaving it to her father and mother to soil themselves by contact with such vulgar matters, so she kept her little secrets to herself: the mustaches of the senior town clerk, the fine figure of the commercial traveler who came once a week to lunch at the Golden Lion, and the blue-eyed gaze of the doctor's son, who never failed to glance up shyly at the embroiderer's casement window when he crossed the street.

She was fifteen, sixteen; she was being brought up, raised, in every sense of the word. She offered no resistance. But she daydreamed too much. And she read too many books—the sugary books that end with princes marrying shepherdesses and governesses marrying English lords. In the feeble light of her bedlamp, lying on her stomach, her elbows propped on her pillow, she grew drunk every evening on stupid stories, which then, stretched out in the dark, she thought about for a long time, twisting a strand of hair around her finger.

Four times a week, she attended classes given by a church school. She walked to school alone, her eyes lowered. She loved

7

literature, the poetry of Lamartine and de Musset and the suff-erings of Andromaque. She sketched skillfully the same pot of flowers from different perspectives, and plaster casts that the instructor had been careful to choose well veiled, well covered. For the most part, science bored her to death, except the natural sciences, which she liked when they were descriptive and had to do with plants. Zoology she detested: the convolutions of the brain and the structure of the kidney reminded her too much of the butcher shop and its bloody displays.

During recreation periods, she kept to herself. Had she not caught her fellow-students snickering as they took scornful stock of her? They belonged to the town's best families, the families of the pharmacist, the tax collector, the registrar of will and probate. Laure watched them walk two by two, clasping each other around the waist; she heard them whispering their secrets. Sometimes she was sorry that her parents were so strict, telling herself that the daughters of the grocer or baker might have liked her. But she considered her isolation a necessary evil, and sometimes she smiled at the vision of how the little hussies would react when her engagement to a prominent young man of the town was announced.

While waiting, she applied herself to becoming educated, so that, as her mother admonished, she would be able to carry on a conversation with no matter who. And although she gave no outward sign, she exulted when the professor read one of her compositions aloud in class.

Because she had no friend to confide in, she had started to keep a diary. She grew tired of it: except for lyrical effusions that came to her after a walk—autumn leaves were always blood-red and golden, sunsets glowing, and fields spangled with tiny flow-ers—she had nothing to write. Her life was so monotonous: nothing ever happened. She was waiting. She hitched her day-dreams to one profile she chanced to see, then to another. In the end, she realized that the succession of aborted little hopes did not deserve to be put down on paper.

Occasionally she wrote poems that she quickly tore up, as if she were ashamed of them. She would turn to her needle again. She sewed, she embroidered sumptuous lingerie that, in gloomy moments, she wondered if she would ever wear.

Come evening, she would clear the table where her father spread out and counted the money earned in the course of the day. She would withdraw to her narrow, bright room. Stretched out on her enameled iron bed embellished with shiny copper balls, she looked more than ever like a big doll of fine porcelain, one of the kind that is no longer made: they used to have real hair and long silken eyelashes, and their eyelids fluttered over pupils of a too intense blue glass.

When—rarely—Mme. Bernardini ventures outside her house, the town bows obsequiously. The town does not hate Mme. Bernardini; it respects her for her position, her wealth, and it likes to recall that the old woman comes from the same clay as do her fellow-citizens.

Mme. Bernardini is reassuring. She is proof that luck does exist, that one can rise in the world provided one perseveres and knows how to seize the day.

IN THE DAYS of Laure's youth, the big house belonged to the richest family in the district. A widow lived in it with her only son.

The widow was stern, corpulent, and dressed always in black. She was, people said, a managerial woman who made life hard for her servants. Her son's name was Paul. As pleasure-loving as his mother was austere, he enjoyed an indolent life, arose late, was negligent in dealing with the tenant farmers who exploited his properties and would have ruined him had not his mother put things to rights. With several boon companions, he went hunting and frequented whores.

His mother was divided between irritation over her son's conduct and admiration for this only child whose charm and affectations in dress delighted her.

People do not remember Paul clearly. A photo in the family album shows him to have been tall, slender, dark-complexioned, with black eyebrows and wheedling eyes; one hand rests casually on a lace-covered pedestal table.

The table still stands in the drawing room of the old house; it is oval, and its satiny mahogany gleams under the light that falls from the tall window. Usually it is supporting some green plant, a potted palm or aspidistra—the plants that often find a place in food shops and perhaps recall confusedly to Mme. Laure's mind the days of her youth.

The hand that rested on the table has long since rotted beneath the earth. Of Paul Bernardini there remains only the photo of an affected fop—and, perhaps, a shred of regret in the heart of his widow. She never speaks of him.

But Mme. Thérèse speaks of him.

She mentions his name in connection with a flower he would have liked, a season he would have found pleasant and good for hunting, or a dish he would have enjoyed. Turning toward Mme. Laure, who watches her through half-closed eyes, she always says "your poor husband" or "your dear departed"; then, in the seemingly strained silence that follows her remark, she heaves a deep sigh and the satin of her bodice squeaks. Mme. Thérèse seems a lapse of taste in the life of Mme. Laure, who is all solemnity and dignity. Mme. Thérèse has rather the appearance of the manager of a house of ill fame. Beneath a reddish wig, worn askew, she has small, laughing eyes, narrow half-moons that are sunk in whitish flesh, surmounted by tinted eyebrows, and underlined by bags. Her nose is flaccid, her chin pointed, her voice vulgar. In the Bernardini household, she seems out of place. She should scarcely have been tolerated in the kitchen, yet she occupies a fine bedroom on the front, and she puts her hand to no work apart from her duties as lady companion; with gracious condescenscion, she allows herself to be waited on by the servants.

On the score of Mme. Thérèse, people murmur that she surely knew how to play her cards, that she brought her ship into port.

What cards did she play, from what port did she set forth, this little old woman who coddles her fat person in the curves of respectable sofas, who gives orders, who permits an expression of cruelty to pass over her face when she is crossed? No one knows, no one knows any more. . . . Eyes become evasive, shoulders are shrugged: it's so long ago; what's to be gained by resurrecting old secrets?

The days pass and are born again. Like worn-out mechanical toys, the old women go to bed, get up, busy themselves with nothings, make slow, vague gestures, in quavering voices exchange small talk that is always, or very nearly always, the same.

Every hour that passes brings them nearer the term of their life.

Their monotonous little comedy would seem pitifully out-of-date, their little outbursts of temper touching and absurd, if, underlying their actions, nourishing their thoughts, one did not divine a stormy past.

Were one to bend over that past, which one thinks one sees trembling like underwater flora glimpsed beneath the depths of glaucous water, could one recognize forms, would one surprise movements? The layers of time, of silence, and of things forgotten compose an almost impenetrable glacis. One is reduced to guessing, to reinventing, in order to understand.

ONCE EVERY SUMMER, the rounded terrace door remains open to the town square, where the ball is being held. Streaked with lights, stippled with colors, the square resembles a kaleidoscope whose patterns form and dissolve. The old women stare out at the square, and it is reflected in the eyeglasses of each. They tell each other that they are fortunate to be able to enjoy the spectacle without breathing in the dust.

But, they say, from their refuge they do not make out the dancers very clearly because their eyesight is no longer good.

They say that this does not much matter. Who knows any of those young people joyously whirling about in the tree-bordered enclosure? Before, it was quite different; one knew the name of every man, every woman, and it was amusing to watch the couples form.

They laugh behind their hands. They stroke their faded old cheeks with their fingers. They keep time with their feet on the stools.

They sniff the scent of their past pleasures in every puff of air that brings them the heavy aroma of caramels and fritters: vanilla and hot oil.

They listen to the blare of the open-air orchestra the way retired sailors would listen to the sound of the sea. Mme. Constantin says that today's tunes are astonishing. Mlle. du Fleuriel says that she thanks heaven for permitting her to have known the waltz and the polka.

Mme. Thérèse says that what counts is to be young and to dance.

The elder Mme. Cygne says, "Youth, youth . . ."

13

The younger Mme. Cygne says that it does not last long, and she sighs.

The beribboned figurines of memory rise, visible-invisible, and there is a silence like the hush that falls, people say, when an angel passes by.

The wind whisks up a handful of confetti that dots the pink flagstones in front of the old ladies.

Mme. Laure says that the introduction of confetti skirmishes into the traditional fête is something new; in the old days, one threw confetti only on carnival nights.

The elder Mme. Cygne finds the innovation regrettable, especially since urchins scoop up their ammunition from the dust and then stuff it even in people's mouths.

Mme. Constantin says that it is a nuisance to find confetti all over everything the morning after the ball.

Mme. Thérèse, rolling her "r"s, says that the year before, she had found one flake—come there who knows in what mysterious way—in the hollow of her bed. She falls abruptly silent. Is Mme. Thérèse thinking perverse thoughts? Is she thinking of the hollow in that bed in which she has slept alone so long? Is she seeing in her mind's eye that stray, that naughty confetti that stuck to her thigh and, dark against her white skin, looked like a beauty mark? She snickers. Mme. Laure frowns.

Mme. Laure says in an undertone that memory is the burden of the old. She stares fixedly at Thérèse's face, which is reddened by the glow from a Bengal light. She shakes her head. She waves her fan in short, rapid strokes. Yet it is not too warm. A breeze is stirring the branches of the syringa and, down below, the lanterns that hang from the plane trees.

Mme. Thérèse blinks mockingly, and her lips purse like the closing of a drawstring bag.

The elder Mme. Cygne is amazed. Is the Coucy boy back from his military service? Certainly that's he dancing with Jeanne Lebon.

The younger Mme. Cygne insists that it is not he, and Mme.

14

Constantin asks whom Jeanne can be dancing with if her fiancé is away?

Mme. Thérèse declares that it is hard to wait when there is a party and one is twenty.

Mme. Laure says in an undertone that Thérèse should know whereof she speaks. Then she breaks off, as if ashamed, and her cheeks flush. She fidgets in her chair, which makes the wicker squeak. She redirects her ill temper against Théodore, her servant-gardener. Why is he not on hand? He must have gone out into the square; he is probably having a drink at the refreshment bar this very instant, when he is needed here.

Mme. Thérèse, suddenly obsequious, says that she will look for him. She gets up, goes over to the ornamental balustrade, and leans out toward the garden. Her rough, cracked voice is heard calling in the direction of the dark mass of trees. Below, something moves. Is it a cat? Is it Théodore? No one answers.

Mme. Laure gestures—too bad, no matter—and Mme. Thérèse returns to her chair.

The music has stopped. The musicians are taking a break and drinking beer on the bandstand. Arm in arm, young people walk back and forth, talking, laughing. The girls have shrill voices. Lovers kiss, mouth to mouth, right in front of the house door. Mme. Laure taps with her foot to chase them away, as one would drive off an importunate animal, but to no avail. Mme. Thérèse says to let them be, they're not hurting anyone.

Mme. Constantin bites on her pastille with a dry crunch. She says that love is a lemon, a bad joke.

Mlle. du Fleuriel asks in a bitter voice if it is better to be deserted, as she had been, on the eve of one's wedding. In her stiff blouse, trimmed at the throat with narrow lace, she does look like a virgin betrayed.

The Cygne ladies sadly recall the two brothers they married on the same day, at midnight, fifty years ago. The best of men they were but, as everyone knows, the good are always the first to go. Mme. Laure says nothing.

15

Mme. Thérèse says that poor M. Paul also went too soon. Then she blows her nose noisily; one would think she is stifling a laugh with her handkerchief. Mme. Laure looks at her with revulsion.

They do not hear the clock strike because of the charivari below, but Mlle. du Fleuriel has a sense of time. She stands up, smooths her skirt, and observes that it is time to go to bed.

Mme. Thérèse turns the key in the lock of the green door. Then she moves to escort Mme. Laure; solicitously, she arranges a fold of her shawl. Mme. Laure shakes her off brusquely. Head high, she steps through the French window, crosses the drawing room, and reaches the vestibule, and, holding herself stiffly, she climbs the stairs without saying good night.

As LONG AGO as the days of Laure's youth, the ball was held on the square with the plane trees. Then, as now, there were benches inside the surrounding wall of trees, but only young people and poor families sat there. For people of quality, chairs were set out beyond the boxwood barriers, and some even preferred to bring their own seats. Laure's mother was one of these.

The streets of the town are on an incline, and the square is situated at a midway point. The evening of the fête witnessed a strange house-moving: a procession of families, each member dragging a straw-bottomed chair with him, would climb up from the lower, or descend from the upper, part of town. Everyone moved slowly, weighed down by his burden but also conscious of marching in a kind of parade, since to arrive with one's own chair was to affirm publicly one's dignity, one's superiority over the bench people.

Laure would hold her stool in one hand and, with the other, lift the folds of her long skirt. She was coming to "watch" the ball: she knew that she would not dance, since her mother forbade her to hobnob with the sons of shopkeepers, and they were the only young men she knew even slightly. Her father, perhaps, would offer his arm for a waltz. The rest of the time, she would have to sit stiffly, back straight, fan herself delicately, and, with a polite smile, decline any invitations that might be offered her. Nonetheless, she had dressed for the evening with care. Was she thinking of Cinderella? Did she dream of some prince in disguise who would notice her?

From where she was seated, she saw only a slow wheeling, a flight of skirts, and sometimes a face she recognized—a schoolmate joyously lifting her high-buttoned shoes to the rhythm of the quadrilles or the polkas. Golden dust rose in the air; the ball seemed to be enclosed within a cloud; Chinese lanterns and girandoles swung back and forth in the light breeze. Below, far away on the bandstand, the clarinet and horn players puffed away, and to one side rose the massive Bernardini house, one door of which stood open, allowing a glimpse of the terrace. Young Laure's glance often rested on this aperture in the night, beyond which one could see the opulent bosom of a tall seated woman and the profile of a young man smoking a long pipe.

The noise and the twinkling lights made little Laure a bit drunk. She envied the dancers, she felt a tingling race up the calves of her legs, she had a mad desire to stand up, to surrender to the rhythm, the movement; unconsciously she beat time with her fan, with her small foot. She used at the same time to say to herself how good it would be to be sitting in the shadow on the terrace of the Bernardinis. She would imagine herself graciously posed on a chair, exchanging well-bred remarks with those distinguished people, putting on airs, and pretending to glance at the festive hullabaloo only out of a sense of duty or because moved to do so by elegant boredom.

Perhaps she wondered why the Bernardini son was not dancing, and instantly she would have answered herself: the common townfolk were not good enough for him. She thought that Madame would have forbidden her son to lower himself by associating with the hoi polloi, and concluded that he was like herself, for she also was being strictly brought up, by Berthe, with a view to a lofty destiny. Or else she did not think at all about Paul Bernardini, never having met him, and was content to survey the austere and imposing façade of the house, which occupied one whole side of the square, and to envy its inhabitants, imagining them to be superior and disdainful.

18

Time passed, dance followed dance, and the musicians mopped their foreheads with big handkerchiefs. Inside the multicolored lanterns, the candles were shrinking and one by one spluttering out. Berthe and Eugène decided that the time had come to go home. And Laure picked up her stool, pinched the pleats of her skirt, not one of which had been mussed. The family walked with measured step down toward the business section of town.

Laure undressed and, with a sigh, went to bed. Abandoned on a chair, her lovely dress gleamed in the light of the moon like a cut flower.

PEOPLE SAY that the first time Mme. Laure met the man she would one day marry was on the occasion of her delivering an order of meat. So one must deduce that the young girl did share somewhat in her parents' business life. Unless one is to suppose that her mother, shrewd fox, sought the custom of upper-class families with a marriageable son and would feign a passing fatigue in order to maneuver her daughter into a meeting. She would instruct her to carry a package to the house in question and, perhaps to rectify the trivial aspect of the transaction, would add to the roast a bouquet of fragrant herbs: fennel, thyme, rosemary, or marjoram.

Thus it was that one morning little Laure, her hair neatly braided, her basket on her arm, walked up to the big house.

She would have had to enter by the servants' entrance and go directly to the kitchen. Did the maid offer her a cup of coffee or some little delicacy? Did she linger a moment? Mme. Bernardini came in. Laure's pleasant manners, her good education, must have beguiled the lady of the house, who invited the girl to accompany her to her bedroom, to show her some chiffon or a bit of lace she had no further use for.

Following Mme. Bernardini, Laure walked down long halls that gleamed with beeswax. Numerous oak doors, all closed, lined the hallways; behind them a mysterious life must be throbbing that had nothing in common with the narrow existence of the butcher's daughter. What was her fifteen-year-old head thinking; what was her little brain, fed on romantic tales, imagining? She was almost afraid of those portals; at the same time, she was stirred by curiosity, she burned to know what rites

20

unfolded behind those dark double doors, to see the décor concealed by those walls and partitions of oak. She imagined it to be sumptuous in form and color. And when Mme. Bernardini led her into her bedroom, Laure was not disappointed.

Mme. Bernardini's bedroom has not changed. Even today, when Laure, who now sleeps there in her turn, has become an old woman, it has the same heavy furnishings, it is hung with the same darkly shining moiré draperies. The curtains fall in stiff pleats, and are caught back by loops decorated with silken tassels. The bed, wide and high, which is reached by steps, half disappears under a multicolored canopy. The highly polished upright desk still holds the family papers, and the marble-top table with its richly, tortuously carved pedestal, has preserved its place before the fireplace, where no fire is ever lighted.

Laure sat down on a low chair—the one still to be seen there, its seat upholstered in tapestry with a design representing a beribboned shepherdess. She looked at the fabrics Mme. Bernardini took from the heavy commode with gilded hinges and knobs. Under the lace, Laure's slender fingers showed a delicate pink. And Mme. Bernardini was astonished by their softness, by the sheen of their nails. She was not to forget the distinction of the little butcher girl.

Laure accepted the lace finery with much gratitude. She was almost drunk, carried beyond herself by the atmosphere of this rich, somber, proud house. She found everything so beautiful that she forgot to appear timid. She looked up at old portraits, their lines blurred by time, with an expression of ravished delight. Even Mme. Bernardini, whom she had always considered displeasing in her role of the competent, superior woman, was invested by these surroundings with a kind of poetry, a grandeur that was no longer overwhelming but venerable. She was like a glorious galleon returned from a voyage, scarred by the vicissitudes of time and tempest, but calm, ennobled by deeds

21

well done; she seemed rightly confident of her strength and the value of her booty.

It was perhaps at this moment that young Paul came in. He bowed to his mother. He was wearing one of his Cashmere dressing gowns of a complicated floral design, loosely tied at the waist by a silk belt. With his dark, shining hair, he resembled a pirate who had been unbraced by luxury. Laure fell in love with him forthwith.

Or else, later, as she was leaving, as she was walking down the hall of the big house, but now in the opposite direction, she saw a door half open, and against an olive-green or plum tapestry background, she caught sight of Paul Bernardini, with the bright eyes and fresh face of a man who has only now finished his toilette. The scent of his eau de Cologne covered that of the wax. He was holding his long pipe with its amber stem. He was smiling, remote. He was the last image Laure took away with her from the big house. He remained in her memory, framed in the doorway, like one of those postcards still to be found on the revolving stands in railway bookshops, the ideal photograph of the seducer.

She began to dream about him. She resumed writing in her diary. It must still exist, that moleskin-bound confidant, in the bottom drawer of the desk or in some trunk with a convex lid now relegated to the attic. Unless young Laure, after becoming Mme. Bernardini, destroyed it one angry day. She recorded her first meeting with Paul. She described him, using the most flowery adjectives. She ventured so far as to imagine that he had noticed her and that, as he smoked his pipe with the amber stem, he would sometimes think of two long braids tied back with a velvet ribbon.

Then phrases that she considered too bold she crossed out, but she knew that they were there, hidden under a stroke of ink, and she caressed them with her finger. Twenty times in a row she wrote, "Paul Bernardini, Paul Bernardini. . . ." And again, with little strokes, she carefully crossed out each line.

22

She changed. Now she was scarcely interested in the movements on the street. If she still glanced out the window, it was in the hope of someday seeing Paul pass by her house. A very slender hope: the young man had little reason to venture into the street of small shops. Other and surely passionately interesting occupations must lead him elsewhere. Did she really want him to come into contact with the paternal butcher shop? If he had appeared, she certainly would have drawn back from her casement window. It was essential that he inhabit an infinitely beautiful and poetic world, whose frontiers he must never cross. She wanted to remain for him a vision scarcely glimpsed, a dream.

Since she thought that they belonged to different worlds, she was sure she would never be able to meet him again. She decided that she would not marry, she would spend her life alone, she would consume herself in honor of Paul Bernardini. She wept over the fate that had decreed she be born a shopkeeper's daughter. She came to detest her parents, whom she judged responsible for her modest station in life. With soft voluptuousness, she thought of suicide. She grew deliciously tender about her unhappiness. Sometimes, when she left school, she would walk to a place in the upper town from which, if one leaned over an old wall, one could catch sight of the Bernardini terrace. Forgetting the time and her mother, who would be worried, she would linger there, casting her pious love over the housetops toward the one who was so far from her. To her, it seemed as if her immense tenderness were descending over the town, covering it like a veil. Once, perhaps, she saw young Bernardini on the terrace. He was patting a dog. She supposed it was his hunting dog, since people claim that Paul was a hunter. He stayed hardly two minutes, then went back into the house, and the dog followed him.

Laure apparently began to take such a fancy to dogs that her father proposed giving her one as a companion. She refused. Her mother shrugged. Laure was becoming hard for her par-

23

ents to understand; often she hurt their feelings; instead of behaving toward them with her customary affection, she now treated them with scorn and irritation. It saddened them. They even wondered whether the education she was receiving, instead of making her grateful, might not one day turn her against them. But it was too late to change course.

Furthermore, except for brief periods of discouragement, Laure's mother pursued her ambitious dream and spent long evenings discussing with her husband the respective merits of sons of "good" families in town. Among them, she hoped to find a son-in-law. Young Bernardini appeared on her list, but at the bottom: of them all, he seemed the most problematical. Despite her desire for glory, Berthe Lambert considered him virtually inaccessible.

PEOPLE SAY Mme. Laure has a bad heart. No doubt that is what gives her those violet lips and faded mauve cheeks. At times, her fleshy throat begins to throb, and she presses her hand against it as if to still the pulsing of her blood and the pain that suddenly wracks her. Mme. Thérèse hands her the little engraved silver box that contains pink pills. She reaches into it with trembling fingers, and then slowly becomes calm again; she smiles, relaxed; the pain has passed.

One wonders how much longer the pills will do their work. Mme. Laure's sons, the doctor and the pharmacist, who live in a distant province and rarely visit their mother, have not concealed from her the gravity of her condition. After each attack, Mme. Laure's smile is a smile of triumph; once again, she has subdued her illness, she has won a fresh reprieve.

Mme. Laure Bernardini, stretched out on her back, hands clasped, feet touching, is resting precisely in the middle of the bed, just as she will lie there on the day of her death for the final lying-in-state. She is not asleep. She has always slept poorly, and age has aggravated her insomnia.

She starts at every noise: the creaking of a chair, the bang of a shutter insecurely fastened. The window, which is left open at this time of year, forms a large bluish rectangle that is scarcely dimmed by the wire-mesh screen. Mme. Laure knows that her nervousness is the prelude to an attack; she divines the pain before she feels it. She turns on the night lamp and searches in the drawer of her bed table for the medication

25

Thérèse should have put there. She does not find it.

Mme. Laure raises herself cautiously. She sits up, uncovers one leg, then the other. She stands up. She steels herself to cross the enormous space that separates her from the wardrobe.

The night lamp forms a luminous bluish cocoon, in the center of which is a single shining point surrounded by concentric, increasingly diffused halos. Beyond their reach, only the pale glimmerings of the moon light the semidarkness and make familiar shapes look unreal: surfaces are moiréd by reflections, objects seem more dense and are deformed by the shadows that prolong and alter them.

Mme. Laure, one hand on her fluttering heart, shuffles slowly toward the wardrobe that looms in the distance. She reaches its smooth, mirrored door, which swings open with a long groan.

Mme. Laure has seized the box. She returns to bed and lies down. She places a pill on her tongue and swallows it with a mouthful of lime-blossom tea.

She feels better. The pincers are opening, and she dares draw a deep breath. She lets her head fall back on the pillow, relaxed.

For a moment, she has dozed off. Now, once again, her eyes are wide open; her skin is irritated by contact with the bed linen; her hands and feet are damp.

She gets up and walks to the window.

The night is calm and clear over the garden. The leaves form a lacy filigree, here black, there silvered by the moon. The little pond shimmers. The gravel paths are as white as milk. An owl hoots, and it seems as if the darkness is about to enfold that cry like sleeping water into which a stone is tossed. Tiny clouds unravel across the sky; they half veil the moon, then pass on, leaving it in its soft, full roundness.

Mme. Bernardini slips into her dressing gown, which has been laid out at the foot of her bed. She leaves the room and walks along the hall. At the top of the stairs, she pauses. She grasps the balustrade and, holding on to it firmly, she slowly walks down, pausing at each step.

The empty vestibule is easily traversed, but in the drawing room the furniture presents obstacles. The lock sticks, but finally turns. The door swings open onto the vaguely pink pool of the terrace, where abandoned chairs resemble a conversation without speakers.

The air is mild. At the foot of the steps that separate the garden from the terrace, the air is gorged with sweet smells, laden with a dampness redolent of friable earth and fallen leaves. Mme. Laure floats along the white path, beside beds of roses that are dark and stiff, like flowers for a cotillion, like velvet ornaments pinned to the bodices of ball gowns, like cemetery wreaths of pearls mounted on circlets of wire.

A forgotten watering can glitters. A rabbit stirs in its sleep and thumps against the side of its cage, which gives off an almost melodious sound. A cricket chirps a tiny, one-note song. The leaves of the boxwood rustle when her dressing gown brushes against them. The gravel squeaks under her slippers.

Since the path encircles a grassy lawn, the stroller returns to her point of departure. She climbs back up to the terrace and lingers there a moment, the only standing, the only human being amid the silence of things. Then she re-enters the house.

The stairs are more difficult to climb than to descend, and the hallway on the second floor is as dark as a tunnel. Thérèse's bedroom opens onto it, and through the closed door a faint snoring is audible. Mme. Laure gently turns the doorknob.

Thérèse is lying on her bed, her mouth agape. The moon is shining down on her and reveals her hair, the hair of a superannuated boy, sparse and as stiff as steel wool.

Mme. Laure laughs soundlessly. She leans over, almost touching Thérèse's body. Then, as if seized by a sudden inspiration, she raises an imaginary rifle to her shoulder and fires several shots at the soft bosom half bared by a flanelette nightgown. She grimaces with distaste at the sight of the blood she has just shed. She shrugs and withdraws silently, as she has come.

The moon is setting. The shadows of objects are lengthening over the carpet, enriching it with bizarre patterns.

Mme. Laure lies down and closes her eyes.

THE SECOND MEETING of Laure and young Bernardini must have offered some elements of drama. A touch of tragedy seems essential to account for the breadth of the girl's passion, and the durability of a memory that Paul was to exhume intact later, in a moment of distress.

Did the meeting take place immediately after the forest fire, which has been the topic of so much talk and in which, it is said, the Bernardini youth almost lost his life?

In setting out as a volunteer to fight the fire, Paul was not acting out of pure generosity: a number of family properties were threatened. However, he could have left the defense of his possessions to others. Hearing that he had sallied forth to face danger, Laure could not help but see him in the guise of a hero.

As time passed—and the wind did not fall—the young girl's admiration gave way to anguish. Daylight faded, and the evening shadows were thickened by a fine ash, slender embers that turned to dust between one's fingers. The stench of burned pitch invaded the town. Laure felt oppressed, but she could no longer tell whether she breathed with difficulty because of the suffocating air or whether anxiety alone was tightening her chest.

As a news account tells it, while fighting the fire Paul clumsily cut his leg with his axe. He had lost contact with his companions, and, surrounded by flames, he had wandered about, bleeding profusely, despairing of making himself heard over the roar of the fire. It was a miracle that he had been rescued.

They had carried him as far as the horse-drawn cart. At the

29

outskirts of town, he had fainted, and because his wound was still bleeding, his companions had refused to take him any farther.

The news story does not specify where the firefighters set their comrade down. May one not assume that it was directly in front of the Lambert shop (Beef—Lamb—Poultry), which was on their route? One imagines the frantic Laure bending over the unconscious youth.

They carried him inside the shop. While awaiting the arrival of his mother, Mme. Bernardini, they bathed his temples with water and vinegar. Laure was supporting his head; every time she moved, a lock of her long hair brushed the injured youth's forehead.

When he opened his eyes again, the first thing he saw, upside down, was Laure's face. He lifted a still unsteady hand and his fingers, soiled with mud and soot, seized the rope of soft hair. Laure shuddered.

They were separated: Paul was borne off in an automobile fetched by his mother. Under eyelids that had closed again, he preserved for a long time, perhaps, the vision of a blanched face and two large eyes filled with tender distress.

Later, Laure many times relived the vicissitudes of that evening up to what for her was the essential moment: the instant when Paul had looked up at her, and his fingers had closed around her hair.

She took the scissors from her embroidery work basket, and she cut off the tress the young man had touched. She preserved it in a locket.

The locket still exists. Mme. Laure Bernardini wears it sometimes. Does she still know that a bit of her own hair is enshrined in it? She doesn't speak of it. Furthermore, faded by time, the hair is neither blond nor brunette; it could have belonged to anyone.

The locket itself is quite handsome. It is an oval fashioned of twisted gold threads set with pearls. The memento is scarcely visible through its tiny clouded glass.

When one looks at the locket resting horizontally on an opulent black-swathed bosom, it is better not to evoke the tender breast of young Laure.

OLD THÉODORE is sitting in the kitchen, all alone, facing the pot into which coffee drips slowly.

It is not quite six o'clock. Mme. Laure has not yet arisen, nor has Mme. Thérèse.

Théodore is muttering to himself. Gala evenings are not good for him any more, he tells himself; they rekindle memories. Because of the general jollity, he lets go on such evenings and drinks more than is wise. Downing one glass of white wine after another, he soon gets a bit tipsy; then visions from the past arise and do not leave him for a long time.

Théodore is like an old book, a closed book; he is like an album from a bygone day, the kind that is secured by a silver clasp. Drunkenness releases the hasp, and the book opens.

Théodore wonders if he will ever be quit of memories. The festive nights he has known, strung on the thread of time, seem to him a series of glass beads. They are a cheap necklace, like the one that night when it all began. Had it not been for that necklace, who knows, Théodore asks himself, what would have happened?

It is useless to daydream: things are as they are. M. Paul is dead. He who thought he was so clever was the first to go. When all's said and done, who does win?

Théodore tells himself that his bed and board are assured for life: that's indeed something. And his youth, his freedom—with time he would have lost them, no matter what. The cards are down, he tells himself. But life is not the same, depending on whether you look at it from this end or that end, whether from its beginning or from its close. If he has won, it's not in the way he would have expected.

Everything changes, gets out of shape—things do, people do. A job you keep, provided you're careful about it, whereas a woman you're sure to lose. Faithful or unfaithful, loving or cruel, she gets away from you, she loses her looks right in front of your eyes; every second, the beautiful fruit rots a little. If you stopped to think about it, you'd be revolted by that decaying flesh.

He tells himself that the game's not worth the candle, that the world's made all wrong, since you eat your cake first—if, of course, you have cake to eat.

He's found very little cake on his table.

And now here he is, an old man. His shoulders are bent, his crooked legs hurt and make him peevish.

What's left for him is a roof over his head and three meals a day. When the album of memories is finally closed, he'll be almost happy, at that. The point is to live from day to day, to enjoy the aroma of coffee and the warmth of summer, which is kind to aching backs.

He tells himself that there is no one he loves. His only friends are the rabbits. He falls silent, for the maid's footsteps are echoing in the hallway. He refills his bowl with coffee.

LAURE'S PARENTS owned a modest property on the outskirts of town, where streets become roads and the last houses change into farms. It amounted to a few rows of grapevines and one small house surrounded by an orchard. The shopkeepers intended to retire there, once their daughter was settled. While waiting, they gave minimal care to their land, which they visited only on Sundays.

Laure, made resourceful by passion, had the idea of going to the orchard to pick some plums and offering them to Paul Bernardini, whose confinement she had learned of from the chatter in the butcher shop. People said that since the fire he hardly ever moved from his chaise lounge because of his wound, which refused to heal.

One does find a trace in elderly people's recollections of the basket of fruit Laure took to young Bernardini. Some claim the hamper contained grapes; others speak of apples or cherries. Given the kind of trees that still grow around the Lamberts' little house, and also the season (the plucking must have followed hard on the fire, which one must place in the summertime), it is reasonable to imagine young Laure arranging some blue plums in her basket, and then covering them with broad vine leaves to protect them against the heat.

Her hamper on her arm, Laure walked toward the Bernardini home. She did not hope to present her offering in person; she did count, at least, on the possibility that the servant who accepted it would think to mention her name when delivering it to Paul. Then, she told herself, as she left she would glance quickly toward the pink terrace, and she might catch a glimpse of Paul stretched out, reading or smoking his pipe. She asked nothing more, slipping readily into a self-effacing role that accorded with her timid nature.

The servant girl had gone out. It was Madame who answered the door knocker. Touched by the girl's act and wishing to give clear proof of her appreciation, she urged her to come out to the terrace to deliver her rustic gift.

Thus it was that Paul and Laure met for the third time.

There is talk of a note that the young man, profiting from his mother's momentary inattention, allegedly slipped into Laure's hand.

Paul would have had to prepare his message long in advance, and he would have had to be waiting for an opportunity to get it to its destination. Seeing that Laure was young and timid, recalling, perhaps, the solicitude she had already shown on his account, without a moment's hesitation he made her his messenger.

Did he offer her a compliment? Did he press her slender wrist as he accepted the basket? He knew how to use the dark eyes he had inherited, so it's said, from an Andalusian forebear.

Laure was able to exert enough self-control to show no part of the agitation that seized her. If she did blush, Paul's mother surely ascribed her heightened color to emotion—most understandable in a shopkeeper's daughter who found herself admitted briefly into the world of high society.

Laure thrust the paper into her pocket. She took her leave, after expressing her wishes for his prompt recovery.

Did she dare believe, if only for an instant, that the note was for her? She had time to imagine a thousand and one follies as she walked along the street leading to her home. The paper burned her skin through the material of her dress; she heard it rustle, and she thought everyone was staring at her, with glances that were mocking or envious or full of commiseration. She walked stiffly, taking care to place her feet firmly on the ground. She was trembling, and she was hot.

35

It was only when she had regained her bedroom that she looked at the note. It was a sealed letter addressed to Thérèse Reboul.

In those days, Thérèse was a person whose name right-thinking people pronounced only with disdain. She lived in the upper town with her mother, an old lady who everyone agreed was repugnant. Thérèse was a milliner. And if the ladies of the town considered her a fallen woman, they nonetheless gave her their patronage. Thérèse was clever with her hands, and she had no equal in winding a ribbon or fluffing tulle or positioning artificial flowers.

Everyone knew (except little Laure, in front of whom such things were never mentioned) that Thérèse was the mistress of young Bernardini.

But understanding comes quickly to girls. Reading the name "Thérèse" on the envelope, Laure had guessed the truth and collapsed on her bed in tears.

Her romance was shattered. She had always thought that Paul was not for her, but to know that he had taken up with another woman seemed to her frightful, and all the more so since, from the social point of view, Thérèse was hardly a catch. Laure could have accepted almost serenely her beloved's betrothal to an heiress. But, she said to herself, if he was going to single out a milliner for his attentions, he could as well have lowered his sights to a butcher's daughter. She no longer considered herself the victim of her modest situation but the victim of cruel chance. She found the injustice of it all unbearable, and there was the added humiliation of having hoped for one moment that Paul's letter was for her. She wept a long time.

One slight consolation assuaged her grief: Paul Bernardini had deigned to charge her with a confidential mission. With a heavy heart, she resigned herself to being no more than a confidante. She promised herself she would perform the role well, although she did not feel at all fitted for it. She was quick, however, to project her unhappiness in a theatrical context; she envisaged herself as Élvire, as Élise, and in this dramatic fantasy she took bitter satisfaction.

The character of Thérèse presented some difficulties, for the milliner would not, she believed, be well cast as Esther or Chimène. However, since she was not acquainted with Thérèse, she could not keep from visualizing her as a persecuted princess; also, since Thérèse was a milliner, Laure forthwith decked her out in veils and diadems. Exalted by the ardor of her love, she began to love Thérèse, only to hate her the next instant. And each passing moment added a richer illumination to the dream image of Thérèse, until her beauty stood out against the gloomy walls of the upper town with the brilliance of a gilded virgin.

MME. THÉRÈSE is sleeping, her mouth pursed as if she were whistling. Her soft, damp flesh exudes a warm, sweetish odor, sweat and perfume commingled.

Théodore wipes his mouth on the back of his hand. He heads for the garden, where his work awaits him.

Mme. Laure gets up.

She rises early: at eight in winter, at seven in summer. She slips on a mauve dressing gown, straightens her nightcap, and walks down the stairs, all the more majestic because her step is slow, burdened by the dreams of the night. The maid hastens to prepare her breakfast tray: the bowl with the violet pattern, two rusks on a saucer, butter, sugar, and a pot of coffee.

Mme. Laure dips her rusks in her bowl and snaps them up, well moistened, just as they are about to crumble; she chews them at length with her remaining teeth. Then she drinks her coffee in long draughts; delicately, she pats her lips with the corner of the napkin. She calls the maid and asks if Mme. Thérèse has come down. The maid replies that she must still be resting, and proposes to go upstairs to see. Mme. Laure acquiesces.

Mme. Laure paces up and down the room. The French window opens onto the terrace and offers a glimpse of the syringa border and the bright, early-morning sky. She waits.

A half-hour passes. Mme. Laure turns, alerted by the slap of worn shoes. Thérèse appears, unkempt, wig askew, eyes bleared, eyelids pasty with sleep.

Mme. Laure exclaims, "Up so soon, my dear?" She remarks

38

that Mme. Thérèse looks poorly, and Mme. Thérèse replies that she slept very little.

Mme. Laure is astonished. From her bedroom she was sure she had heard snoring. . . . Mme. Thérèse protests. She was not snoring. Her nose was stuffed up; it was cool last night out on the terrace, and her shawl—Mme. Laure does not allow her to finish. She says that if Thérèse wanted to sleep the morning away, she could say so, and certainly no one would have disturbed her. She declares that she does not need Thérèse every hour of the day. At times, she enjoys solitude, and she considers herself alert enough still, God be thanked, to get along for a few moments without a maid. She adds that Thérèse, at her age, needs a long night's rest.

Mme. Thérèse turns red and stammers a furious reply that does not escape clearly through the barrier of her dentures.

Mme. Laure, all serene, goes out into the garden for her morning constitutional.

Mme. Thérèse asks for her breakfast. She stuffs herself on slices of bread and butter with a vengeance.

Mme. Laure walks slowly along the gravel path. She passes in front of the rabbit hutches. Théodore is there, changing the litter. As Mme. Laure passes by, he straightens up and, holding his pail filled with droppings, with his free hand he gives a military salute. Mme. Laure nods to him condescendingly and moves on. She makes the "tour of the garden." She leans down to straighten the stem of a lily, and picks off a snail, which she crushes under her heel.

She has come back, full circle, to the house. She goes up to her room to dress.

IT WAS already the beginning of autumn. The sky was tinged with pale purple, objects were losing their sharp outlines, and a slightly muggy mildness made everything torpid.

Or, indeed, summer was reigning still, and the sun, having to traverse a long portion of its orbit toward the horizon, hardened every façade, disclosed the texture of every stone, and sent blue shadows flowing along the narrow alleys bordered by houses to which it gave, in contrast, a reddish cast. The streets twisted steeply upward, and as Laure plodded on they grew more and more narrow, older and older. Her step slowed as she came near Thérèse's house. She pressed her little handbag against her hip and lifted her chin, but her lips were trembling.

People say that the milliner's shop used to be located by the town walls. The street ended there; a solitary oak reared up, a kind of sentinel planted at the limits of town and hill.

If autumn had begun, a few fallen leaves were swirling about in a sudden gust of wind. Laure clutched her shawl, which threatened to blow away; evening was falling, and the inhospitable neighborhood rebuffed the young girl. The milliner's shopwindow was glistening, either because a lamp had been lighted or because the last rays of the sun were playing over two mannequin heads, with painted eyes and hats beribboned in tulle and decorated with roses or cherries. In the background, Thérèse could be seen bent over her work, thrusting her long needle into the straw or velvet.

Laure pushed the door open. She paused on the threshold, at the light tinkling of the doorbell. That is how Thérèse first saw her: slender, pretty, frightened yet resolute. With a practiced eye, she assessed her visitor's figure, face, and hair. She bit her lip: she did not like a woman to be prettier than she.

At the same time, Laure was observing Thérèse, astonished to find her small and vulgar, surprised by the pallor of her complexion and the circles under her eyes. Was this the woman Paul was languishing for? The gilded statue, the virgin of the diadems, gave place to a common workingwoman utterly lacking in style. Artlessly Laure told herself that all was not yet lost: against such a rival she felt she could fight, could conquer. The inaccessible Paul, by dint of his interest in an ordinary milliner, was descending from his heights; he was drawing nearer to Laure. He was becoming a man one could hope to win.

Laure's eyes were adjusting to the light in the shop. She made out the confusion of materials tossed here and there, and piles of open cardboard boxes; the paint on the walls was faded and scaling; the mirrors were tarnished. Unaware of the expression of disdain that flashed across her face, Laure was weighing, calculating her chances. She forgot her timidity and even the reason that had brought her there. Finally, Thérèse inquired about the purpose of her visit. Wordlessly, Laure held out the letter. Thérèse read it, while with her free hand she tucked in a wisp of hair that had escaped from her chignon, then sucked her thumbnail. She began to smile. She folded the letter and slipped it in her pocket. Laure waited. Thérèse said there was no reply.

THÉODORE has finished cleaning out the hutches. He takes advantage of the maid's absence to go to the kitchen and put a mash of uncooked bran on the stove to simmer. Leaning over the range, he stirs the dark muck with a big wooden spoon. This is how the maid finds him. She scolds: one more casserole that will be ruined. Théodore says that he has found a dietetic recipe for his rabbits in the almanac: selected herbs mixed with ox blood, a dash of flour, spices. . . . The big speckled rabbit is about to throw her young, and he plans to try out the merits of the fortifying brew on her. The maid sighs, and Théo continues to push the spoon through the mixture, which is thickening and swelling; blisters bulge on the surface and, bursting with tiny exhalations, cast off scalding drops. A stale, nauseating smell issues from the casserole, spreads even as far as the living quarters, and assails the nostrils of Mme. Thérèse.

Mme. Thérèse has a sensitive nose and, at this hour of the morning, a quick temper. She tracks down the source of the smell, erupts into the kitchen, and berates Théo. He bends lower. He draws figure eights with his spoon, and remains silent. Mme. Thérèse becomes exasperated and her voice rises, grows shrill, and cracks. Théo looks Mme. Thérèse straight in the face and laughs.

The maid has withdrawn to the other side of the kitchen. She pretends to be busy scouring pots, but from the corner of her eye she is watching, half curious, half frightened.

Mme. Thérèse snatches up the casserole and hurls it to the floor, where the dark-brown gruel spreads out in wide, smoking streams.

The maid cries out, then falls silent. And Thérèse, who has recovered her breath, yelps that Théo is clumsy; it's bad enough to cook some filthy porridge or other in the house, but to spill it on a freshly scrubbed floor is the end.

And while Théo crouches down to mop the floor, she withdraws, chewing a cud of vengeful satisfaction.

The maid shrugs. As he washes the tiles, Théo groans.

IF ONE takes into account the education Laure had received and the novels she had immersed herself in, it is clear that the young girl was quite incapable of conceiving of any difference between love and desire. Did she even suspect the existence of carnal pleasure? She appears to have been more cerebral than sensual; indeed, her history seems to show that she was very close to being a frigid woman. If in this her husband was somewhat at fault, there was also, no doubt, her own innate predisposition.

A different upbringing could have transformed Laure. But in the days of her youth—and, indeed, long after—pure, cold young women, carefully brought up to remain pure and cold, were thrown into marriage as Christian virgins were once exposed to the bulls. It was up to them to awaken, to adapt, or to become resigned.

For Laure, love meant marriage. She continued to be convinced that young Bernardini wanted to marry the milliner; the very idea astonished her, grieved her. But, she told herself, the marriage had not yet been celebrated. If Paul found a little tradeswoman acceptable as a wife, Laure estimated that a butcher shop was as good as a hat shop, and she began to lose her sense of inferiority, especially because she had found Thérèse very ordinary. She decided she would win the Bernardini heir.

One can ask oneself, Did ambition not play a part in Laure's wish to marry Paul?

She had loved the young man naïvely, stirred by his fine appearance, by the luxury that surrounded him, by the reputa-

44

tion of his family. That luxury, that wealthy, proud house rearing up in the heart of town—did they not account for much of the little butcher girl's tender passion? Would she have loved Paul had he been no less attractive but the son of a road repairman? Unbeknownst to her, Laure had been contaminated by her mother's dreams of glory, conditioned by them in some way, and she could no longer separate a man's charm from his position. Paul had everything: he was the well-dressed, perfumed family scion, heir to a long family lineage, descendant of a respected tribe; his wealth counted as much as the fire in his eyes; his silken dressing gown was quite as much a part of his person as was his black hair. One would no doubt have shocked Laure had one insisted with her that if by mischance ruin had befallen her beloved, he would have scarcely mattered to her any more. But no such eventuality was to be feared. In the novels she had read, it was always the girls who were the victims of poverty, and they always ended up marrying well-off young men. This was the reward for their love, their virtue, their patience; this re-established an ideal order.

In aspiring to an alliance with young Bernardini, Laure was conforming at once to the wishes of her parents and to models she did not dream of criticizing. With a clear conscience, she set about hatching a plan.

Paul, however, was impatient at receiving no reply to his letter, and he had decided he would contrive to have the young girl return to his house. Since he was subject to the authority of his mother, whom he twisted around his little finger but never faced up to, he had to resort to a ruse. Exaggerating his prostrate condition, he asked if someone would be so kind as to come read aloud to him; he was reduced to staring the whole day long at the narrow horizon of the terrace; he was bored.

Mme. Bernardini suggested various readers. He responded to each name with a pout, a shrug. Just as Madame was beginning to fear he would propose the name of the milliner, she was

45

relieved, almost happy, to hear him mention the young girl of the plums. She promised to find out as soon as possible whether the girl would be a possible reader. Her fears allayed, she went off and Paul sank back, content, against his cushions.

Laure became, for a short time, the young man's paid companion.

PAUL must have been disappointed to see Laure arrive empty-handed. Thérèse had given her nothing? Laure shook her head. Did Paul permit himself to show some sign of doubt? Did he throw out the suggestion that the girl had failed in her mission? He was obliged to surrender to the evidence when Laure related, in great detail, her expedition to the upper town.

She had grown more self-assured; she expressed herself well, and, chagrined as he was, Paul could not fail to admire her. What was he, after all, but a lout? Laure could have observed that, his position apart, Paul was worth less than she. If she did not, it was because love continued to blind her.

She was holding the book she was supposed to read aloud—an essay on bream fishing. She was amazed to have covered so much ground in so little time. Was she not sitting on the pink terrace, alone in the company of the handsome Paul? She owed the favor she was enjoying to the charms of another, but at last, introduced into the house, approved as a companion to the invalid, it seemed to her that future developments depended on her own skill. Prudently, she took care not to show her infatuation; she conducted herself like a good companion—even like an accomplice—without, however, abandoning a respectful manner. She spoke of Thérèse in measured terms, not denigrating her but trying to put her in her proper place. If she spoke of the milliner's charm, she slipped in an allusion to her indifferent figure; she praised the elegance of the hats displayed in the shopwindow, and regretted that they were not shown to better advantage by being more tidily arranged. Paul did not even defend his mistress. He kept asking over and over why she had failed to answer him. Patiently, Laure offered many explanations, which he seemed to believe only to reject them furiously a moment later.

Madame came frequently to cast an eye on the terrace to make sure that everything was going as it should. Laure would hastily resume her reading, but at random, and so got the impression that the bream was a leaping fish that swam now upriver, now down, fleeing between two pools so often and for such long periods that fishermen must never be able to trap it.

After an hour of interrupted confidences and halieutic instruction, Laure stood up: the convalescent must not be overtired. She was leaving, and Paul should expect her tomorrow. He slipped her another note addressed to Thérèse.

Laure delivered the second missive as she had delivered the first.

Thérèse was out, and Laure had to wait quite some time in the shop, where a scurvy old woman puttered about, dabbing here and there with a sour-smelling cloth and groaning the while. When the milliner came in and saw Laure, she raised her eyebrows. The messenger missed no nuance of Thérèse's grimace of irritation. She asked for a reply, and Thérèse scribbled a few words on a slip of paper torn from her order book. She held out the paper with a laugh that was almost insulting. From a corner of the shop, the old woman watched, open-mouthed. Laure fled.

MME. LAURE'S TOILETTE is no small matter. She indulges in rapid ablutions by herself, but she cannot get dressed without help; her corpulence makes every movement painful and uncertain. As soon as she has bathed, she rings for Thérèse.

Mme. Thérèse climbs the stairs without haste. She finds her mistress standing in her camisole and, with ill grace, undertakes to slip on her heavy black silk dress. For a moment, Mme. Laure's head is lost in the folds of the dark material, and her arms flail about, seeking the sleeves. Finally, her hands free themselves from the tangle, her face emerges, and Mme. Thérèse tugs on the skirt to make it come down. The bodice, which is closed at the back by a long row of tiny jet buttons, must then be fastened. Thérèse has pointed nails, and each buttonhole gives her an opportunity to jab the fat back through the linen of the camisole. Mme. Laure groans, but a few sighs also escape her: half pleasure, half pain.

Then Mme. Laure sits down and extends her feet. Kneeling, Thérèse slips on her stockings one after the other; once toes and heels are adjusted, she draws the mesh up and stretches it over the flaccid calves, their dry skin creased like tissue paper and laced with bluish veins. As she attaches the stocking tops to the garters that span the heavy white thighs, she wrinkles her nose.

Thérèse slips Mme. Laure's shoes on her feet and laces them. Now garbed from head to foot, encased in satin with bronzelike glints, Mme. Bernardini resembles an enormous potbellied scarab. She looks at herself in the mirror, inspects her collar, fastens a brooch at the décolleté point of her gown. At a gesture

49

from her, Mme. Thérèse fetches her batiste cape and her hair-brushes.

Mme. Laure's hair must once have been beautiful. It is still luxuriant, although faded and dry; it is a white forest from which all sap has gone, and through which Thérèse moves her skillful, sometimes cruel, fingers. It seems that the clumsy brushstrokes, the pulls, and the pricks are more or less frequent depending on whether Thérèse has spent a good or a bad morning. Does Mme. Laure lend credence to her lady-in-waiting's explanations: "That was a knot. . . . Your hair is full of electricity today. . . . Ah, the hairpin slipped from my fingers. . . . This comb is scratching your scalp. You should get a new one. . . ."

Sometimes Mme. Laure protests, and lifts a hand to ask for a respite. Then Mme. Thérèse interrupts her work, plumps her pudgy person down on a couch, and reports on the small happenings of the day to that point.

The maid has bought a roast that is far too big; is she feeding her entire family at the expense of the household? Théodore is the limit; he lives only for his rabbits, and he comes indoors to stink up the house with his mash. Mlle. du Fleuriel crossed the square, carrying a letter; she must have written again to that nephew who has an eye on his inheritance—obviously—and doesn't care a whit about her; she was wearing her old yellow cape; as rich as she is, should she not dress decently?

Mme. Laure answers in monosyllables, or not at all. She seems to disdain Thérèse's chatter. Yet if the reporter falls silent, Mme. Laure revives the conversation with a word or two, and Thérèse takes off again. She has managed to find out (how, she does not say; she never gives her sources) with whom Jeanne Lebon was dancing the night of the ball; it was that young man down from Paris on vacation.

Mme. Laure says that Parisian men enjoy prestige in women's eyes. Mme. Thérèse emends: it is not so much the glamour of the capital that beguiles them but the attraction people have who come from somewhere else. Mme. Thérèse gets to her feet, picks up the brush again, and resumes stroking the heavy hair with hands that have grown more gentle. Mme. Laure's neck relaxes, and her head rolls on the upholstered chairback. She closes her eyes. She is like an elderly cat being stroked; now and then she shivers, the cape trembles on her bosom, and a wave of voluptuousness sets the down on her cheeks atremble.

Thérèse has fallen silent. Noises from the street, from the garden, reach the bedroom muffled and expire in the folds of the draperies. The bedroom is a lined chest crammed with precious old objects, tightly closed; a subdued daylight envelops the two women, one standing, the other seated, who appear entirely possessed by a magical game.

Abruptly, Thérèse destroys the charm by yanking on a lock of the white hair. Roused from her ecstasy, Mme. Laure cries out and opens her eyes. Above her, she sees a sneer on Thérèse's face; for a moment, she oscillates between dream and reality, between the beatitude just ended and the animosity reborn.

With a vigorous stroke of the comb, Thérèse traces a part that runs from forehead to neckline. She smoothes the bandeaux, she rolls, she pins. Then she presents the mirror, which Mme. Laure seizes, inclines to left, to right, and returns without a word.

Thérèse removes the cape, shakes it out, and places it in a drawer.

Mme. Laure, shivering again, walks over to the big mirror that hangs above the fireplace. She looks at herself pensively, her elbows propped on the cold marble. Behind her in the mirror, enclosed with her image in its verdigris, gold-flecked depths, is the reflection of Thérèse. They stand motionless, the eyes of the one fixed on those of the other through the intermediary of the reflection. They seem to be holding time still, to be sinking into a stale and senile eternity.

PAUL appeared far from pleased as he read the milliner's scribble. Laure watched him uneasily. If Paul decided to be angry with Thérèse, he would no longer need a go-between; it irritated Laure to have to hope that he would preserve his attachment to her rival.

She did not dare pick up the fishing manual, which lay on her knees, its leaves riffled by the wind. The hour passed in a surly silence. When Madame came out on the terrace, Paul, looking sulky, indicated to her that the reading definitely interested him no longer and that henceforth he would dispense with companionship.

Laure was mortified. He had thought of her only as a tool. Now that he had no further need of her, he was sending her away, and he did not even trouble to warn her; he conveyed the fact of her dismissal through a third person, speaking of her as if she were not there. She got to her feet, scarlet with embarrassment. He bent his head over the abandoned book; with a fingernail, he scratched a color reproduction of that bream young Laure was beginning to detest. She was to retain a distaste for fish that amounted to nausea and, on fast days, led her to eat nothing but eggs and milk.

Mme. Bernardini seemed put out. She escorted Laure to the door, showering her with amiabilities, trying to make excuses for her son: he was indisposed; confinement weighed so heavily on him that it was changing his nature. . . . Laure, heavyhearted, pressed her lips together. When Madame sought to compensate her, she shook her head. She walked away, holding herself upright, and thoughtfully Mme. Bernardini watched the graceful figure cross the square.

Laure's humiliation at being dismissed by young Bernardini without explanation was only the first of such humiliations that she was to endure at the hands of this man who, under the exterior of a provincial dandy, was a boor. One imagines that this was the first step in blazing the road that would lead little Laure far. Closed and secretive, yes, but notwithstanding her childishness Laure was not harebrained. Without her realizing it, her character was being forged; she was acquiring a truer sense of herself and of others. Paul's gross rebuff did not kill but it did alter her love for him.

She had no further contact with Paul for a long time, not until well after the affair of the necklace.

Many rumors have circulated about this incident. Each is different: according to some people, the necklace was a gold chain that Paul had given his mistress and that she had dared to return to him. Other people said that the necklace—a shoddy, cheap necklace—had been offered Thérèse by the traveling salesman who had taken Paul's place in the milliner's bed. For still others, the necklace was a precious piece of jewelry, a part of the Bernardini patrimony, and Thérèse had demanded it in return for dismissing the peddler and bestowing her favors on Paul once more.

Lacking irrefutable proof to accredit this or that version, one has simply to choose. The second hypothesis seems the most likely.

One can imagine Paul Bernardini, barely recovered, still limping but impatient to rejoin Thérèse, slipping out of the house at nightfall.

No doubt he had gone out without telling his mother; no doubt, also, intuition had alerted the latter or concern had made her watchful, and she would have been peering through the slats of the venetian blinds as he left. People say she maintained a constant surveillance over him—a complete waste, since she could prevent nothing—and that she was in the habit of staying awake until he returned home, alone in her great bed, straining for the slightest sound until the small hours of the night.

He gently drew back the bolt of the main door and slipped into the darkness of the town.

The streets were poorly lighted, but he knew the way. Clumping along, cursing his leg, which pained him, he reached the upper town, not without hearing along the way, perhaps, an ironic song *de genre*—"He who gives chase loses his place," or "When you held the quail in your hand was the time to pluck it"—fall from a half-opened window behind which stirred the shadow of one of those busybodies who know everything and who play the bird of ill omen in small towns.

The shopwindow was dark. As was his habit, Paul rapped on Thérèse's shutter. After a moment, she came to open. She was in a nightgown, and her hair glistened. Paul quickly swung a leg over the sill and jumped into the room. Disorder reigned, no doubt, as around Thérèse it always did: stockings trailed from a chair, a stack of hatboxes was threatening to collapse, a skirt and a work jacket lay in a heap on the floor.

Paul saw none of this. He threw himself on the bed, dragging Thérèse, who had not said a word, with him. He took her on the mussed, untidy sheets. He had no idea whether he was giving her pleasure, and cared less. His eyes were shut; he imagined Thérèse's body to be a long shuddering river in which he was swimming, pressing onward along branches of clear water that extended farther and farther. Then Thérèse was a lively, smooth-bellied fish that thrashed and twisted free from his hands. She was an aqueous grotto overgrown with moist, fluid grasses; he forced an entry and discovered the cave carpeted with retractile algae sweating slime, smelling of mud and shells.

54

The river was cold; the cave was swept by broad, hot currents; the water swelled in eddies that seized the swimmer and sucked him into a wild gyration. Waves boomed ceaselessly; the noise bored into Paul's ears until he longed to cling to the walls of the cavern, to hoist himself out of his pleasure; then, with exquisite pain, he consented to let himself die. When he finally withdrew from his mistress, he threw himself, gasping, on the side of the bed and looked at her: she was like sleeping water. He asked her if she had felt pleasure. She propped herself up on an elbow and laughed.

It is true that she was not pretty, but, undressed as she was, her white body leaning against the pillow, her hair disheveled, and her heavy breasts shaken by laughter, she looked like a female devil. He tried to fling himself on her; she pushed him away. She went into the kitchen to look for two glasses and a bottle of wine. She filled the glasses and lifted hers: to their reunion. They drank; they talked. Paul made some reference to his two letters; she replied that writing was not her strong point. They drank again; they caressed each other.

In the adjoining bedroom, Thérèse's mother must have been all ears. Thérèse paid no heed to that; she did not even lower her voice. At last, Paul put on his clothes. It was growing late and he had to leave. It was then, while looking for his pipe, that he saw the necklace.

It was lying in a small bowl on the bed table. It was a necklace of no value, a string of multicolored glass beads on a brass wire long enough to go several times around Thérèse's slender throat. On the little marble tabletop, it glittered like a pretty snake. Paul asked absently where this necklace, which he wasn't familiar with, came from. Thérèse might have said that she had bought the necklace or that she had made it herself, and the matter would have stopped there.

But she had had too much wine; she had felt frustrated by Paul's long absence, perhaps, and humiliated not even to have had the right to go ask after him. Deliberately, she caused the storm to break: she said that a friend, a man, had given her the necklace.

Paul asked who the friend was, and Thérèse repeated that he was a friend. Hadn't she the right to have a man friend? He thought she did not have that right.

Had she, then, only the right to wait? Yes, he had written to her; he had even had her brought two notes by a pretty girl, who could, apparently, visit him whenever and as often as she liked. But, Thérèse wanted to know, what good was a note to a woman left alone? Is it notes that a person needs when she sleeps by herself? She was Thérèse the pestiferous, the leprous. Very well, that had its good side; it meant that she need feel responsible to no one; since she was known as every man's woman, she would grant her company to no matter who.

Was that when Paul saw red? Or did he still try to parley, to unscramble the true from the false, reality from boasts? Being what one knows him to have been—or what one thinks one knows him to have been—he must not have contained himself long before flying into an insane rage.

From the swimmer in the river, from the pursuer of the bream, he was transformed into the hunter: a booted man, smelling of leather and wild animals, who advances with great strides, crushing the bracken, trampling down the high grass, who desires the game as much as the death of the game. It is out of love that one kills deer and doves, in order to possess them for that one instant when the heart of the hunter and the heart of the hunted beat in unison, when the blood of the beast and the sweat of the man seal a dolorous and desperate passion.

Paul seized the doe by the throat; he twisted it, bruised it; he sank his nails in the flesh of the panting doe, while he bit her muzzle, licked her froth, drank the sweat of her agony. And his maddened glance plunged into the eyes of the doe, which bulged and turned glassy. He hurled his victim back on the bed. He placed the ridiculous necklace around her neck.

It was about three in the morning, so runs the gossip, when the neighbors of Thérèse heard cries. They were poor people, fearful creatures. At first they waited in the dark, frozen with terror, imagining horrible tragedies. Finally, they came timidly out of their houses, lighting their way with lanterns. They found the milliner's mother in a crumpled work jacket, her gray hair bristling with curlers; she was calling for help.

In the bedroom, Thérèse lay unconscious. A cheap necklace, was pressing into the white flesh of her neck, which was covered with purple stains. Drops of blood joined the glass beads and, in the half-light, provided the young woman with a sumptuous ornament that extended down to her breasts. She was naked.

Young Bernardini, pale as death, was standing in a corner of the room staring at his hands.

THE BIG SPECKLED RABBIT has dropped her young sooner than Théodore expected. One of her bunnies is dead.

Théo contemplates the tiny cadaver stretched out on the palm of his hand: hairless blue body, soft ears, flat muzzle, closed eyes.

The old man lays the inert shape on the ground, and he undertakes to console the mother, who, frightened, is huddled against the wall, concealing under her belly her other offspring, which have burrowed beneath the straw. Théo searches about in the dirty litter, soiled by glair and blood. Under his fingers, he feels the warm wriggling of little animals whose skin is too delicate. He strokes the big rabbit's flank.

He seems to experience a kind of sensuous pleasure in rubbing down the damp fur, which here and there is matted, and in breathing in the smell of lymph and urine in the hutch. Little by little, the body of the big rabbit abandons itself to the rough hand passing back and forth over its smooth belly. And Théo talks.

A funereal chant issues from him, the words of which have less meaning than does the monotonous croon, which is as soothing as a litany.

Théodore speaks of the sufferings of the rabbit, alone and in the dark when she brings her young into the world. He hopes that she has not suffered too much. He says that Mme. Laure—she, too, knew pain in the darkest of dark shadows. He says that they must have lighted lamps, but that, for him, everything took place in deep night. He says, however, that, he thought he saw the woman quartered on her bed, and that streams of blood gushed from between her legs. He says that he will never forget the smell of the bedroom, the racket of pots of hot water, the clatter of basins, pans, pitchers. And the screams.

He says that for Mme. Laure and the rabbit it's all the same, and that one has to suffer. He says that Mme. Laure and the rabbit are alike, both of them delivered of a dead child. He says that the rabbit is beautiful and that three little ones are left to her.

He says that M. Paul walked up and down, smoking his pipe, and that old Madame called on the Holy Virgin for help. He says that Mme. Laure's mouth was black in her white face, and that they had to strap her arms and legs to the bedposts.

He says that in such moments men are useless: if he had been near the cage when the rabbit was in labor, he would have been of no use.

He says that no one is of any use in times of sorrow. He says that the rabbit will soon be well again, and that Mme. Laure spent days between life and death.

He says that it is better to be a rabbit than a woman, because if one is a rabbit one does not know what death is.

He says that Mme. Laure's blood soaked the sheets. He says he will bring some fine grass to the rabbit, and that her little ones will be handsome and strong.

He says that everything is the fault of Thérèse, who frightened Mme. Laure and overturned the casserole of gruel.

He says that Mme. Laure's hair hung down until it touched the floor, and that the rabbit's coat, once she has cleaned it well, will be smooth and shiny again.

He says that he will bury the little body in the garden. Child or baby rabbit, the difference is not great: every corpse deserves burial.

He goes off, pushing the wheelbarrow on which the tiny

corpse lies, hairless and blue. He is gravedigger, grieving family, and blesser of the grave, all in one.

The crunch of the wheel on the gravel makes a shrill music; the hearse jolts, and a swarm of flies follows on behind.

PAUL BERNARDINI'S INTEMPERATE ACT received front-page attention in the press. The day after the incident, the local paper devoted several columns to it; on the left, it showed the guilty man, haggard, being led away by two policemen; on the right the bold face of Thérèse. The article, written by the town-hall secretary, who was also a press correspondent, expressed profound affliction: its author portrayed the dismay caused the entire town by the inexplicable fall of Paul Bernardini, the scion of an unsullied family line. The writer attacked Thérèse violently; he charged her with all manner of sins, and accused her of having deliberately provoked her lover's insane rage in order to destroy that which she could not equal.

The account was so biased that, years later, reading the recital of the misfortune that long stained the reputation of the Bernardinis, one is led to pity Paul and his mother, not the strangled girl.

Strangled she was not, or not entirely, for Thérèse had fainted from terror before her breath was cut off.

Thanks to her vitality and the energetic, if ungentle, care of the nuns in the poorhouse hospital, the young woman survived and Paul was spared the worst. He was charged with "acts of violence that did not cause death and that were without murderous intent." Defended by a lawyer from among his relatives, who did not fail to blacken Thérèse's name, he was acquitted.

Nonetheless, the Bernardini escutcheon had lost its luster. Paul had been let off, his mother had been pitied, Thérèse had been spat upon. But because Paul had been "haled into court," everyone in town turned his back on him.

People reproached Paul less for his violent act than for his loose living. Known before to all and sundry, the facts had now been spread out in broad daylight: no one could pretend any longer not to know what everyone had been able to read in the paper. People greeted Paul only if they were forced to, caught by surprise before they had time to cross over to the other side of the street. As for Mme. Bernardini, she harvested many a commiserating glance, but people no longer invited her. If she called at homes where theretofore she had been cordially received, servants were instructed to say that the master and mistress of the house were absent and to suggest that she leave her card.

Many people, no doubt, were affecting a reprobation they scarcely felt. Their scandalized airs primarily signified revenge: they were taking advantage of the opportunity to heap scorn on a family they had been obliged until then to respect.

Mme. du Fleuriel, a friend of long standing, was one of the few people who dared still frequent the Bernardini house. After nightfall, she would venture as far as the pink terrace. Together with Mme. Bernardini, she bemoaned the customs of the day and the lamentable evolution of a youthful generation that knew neither religious faith nor respect for the law.

People say that at one time Mme. du Fleuriel had considered arranging a marriage between her daughter and Paul Bernardini. The union would have been advantageous to both parties, but Paul had dug in his heels. He refused to consent, alleging that he had plenty of time "to put his head in the noose," and that the presumptive fine future was not all that fine.

The friendship that bound Mme. Bernardini and Mme. du Fleuriel was not so deep that the latter refrained from gloating. She spoke out; she deplored Paul's unhappy fate, for what decent girl would want to have anything to do with him now? She thereby contrived to suggest that she would reject an alliance that had actually been unwanted by Paul.

Mme. Bernardini swallowed all such bitter pills without losing her queenly manner. But she must have had many worries. And Paul was of no help to her; he marched a dour face from house to garden and back. People claim that he did not seem to be the least bit contrite, and even regretted that Thérèse had recovered. He went so far as to accuse his mother of having caused the wretched affair by her intransigence.

It seems that around this time Paul took a trip. On the pretext of fortifying his uncertain health, Madame sent him, people say, to Italy. He remained there for a month, wandering from city to city, collecting dubious adventures and spending a fortune. Madame summoned him home. He returned, afraid that his funds would be cut off. He had tasted freedom, known the carefree, expansive life of a rich tourist; the big house must have looked small to him on his return.

The town still held itself aloof. Some thoughtful souls informed him that Thérèse, now fully restored to health and more dashing than ever, had become the mistress of an innkeeper. She had given up hats—the women in town no longer ordered from her, on account of the scandal—and she was being kept. She had just put her house up for sale, thus forcing her mother to take refuge in the poorhouse.

It was autumn. Paul never unclenched his teeth, he smoked pipe after pipe, and he glared scornfully at the melancholy garden and the dignified, old-fashioned house.

The days grew shorter and the evenings longer, during which mother and son, sitting motionless and morose on either side of the fireplace, seemed to be keeping vigil for someone who had died.

THÉODORE has buried the baby rabbit behind a row of box-wood.

He has planted a cowslip cutting on the grave. He has gone back to the hutches.

He is all alone, sitting on a wooden bench, knees spread wide, hands hanging limp. His lips move but no sound comes out. The big rabbit is nursing her infants and nibbling on greens. Théo gets up and goes to tap on the screen. But the rabbit is too occupied and does not look at him. He shrugs and moves off. He ventures as far as the terrace, where he can see Mme. Laure and Mme. Thérèse seated at either end of the long table. They are talking, no doubt; Théo sees their heads and hands move. He shakes with laughter at the sight of that pantomime. Since they will not hear him any more than he hears them, he risks addressing them.

To Thérèse's back he says that she is worse than a shrew. He says that Mme. Laure, who gives herself airs, puts up with her because she does not dare throw her out.

He says that he knows her nasty little secrets: how she upsets casseroles of gruel, how she scatters pins in the creases of the cushions, how she traps flies in the china sugar bowl, how she empties her chamber pot every morning at the base of the rosebushes.

He says that he will kill her.

He says that he should have done it before.

He says that she frightens him.

He says that she will bury them all, the way she buried M. Paul.

He says that men live too long; animals live less long.

He sees that the women are rising from table, and he hides behind the syringas.

LAURE had resumed her monotonous life, which no dream of ideal love would ever again illumine. She believed she was advancing slowly toward a proud celibacy; mentally, she declined all the offers that no one made her, declined all the rich and handsome young men who passed beneath her window and scarcely gave her a thought. The son of the ironmonger, on the other hand, lost no opportunity to pay her court. She forgave him. Could he divine the deep despair that was eating her heart away? She even experienced a delicate and perverse pleasure in inflicting on another person some of the pain she was enduring. Often when she was alone she wept, staining her endless handiwork with fat round splotches. Or else she sat motionless and vacant-eyed, and she would see Paul's face in the clouds of sunset, in the intertwinings of branches, in the design of the carpet.

Occasionally, she met Mme. Bernardini as she was setting out for school. Madame chose the early-morning hours to go out, dreading to detect the murmurings or pitying glances that people exchanged as she passed by.

The first time Mme. Bernardini saw Laure after what she called "the tragedy," she scarcely recognized the girl. Laure had grown thin and pale; the adolescent had become a woman, for the months were passing and sorrow matures.

Laure bowed deeply. Surprised by an attitude so unlike that of others, Mme. Bernardini recognized the plum-bearer, the ephemeral reader. She smiled.

One can only guess which of them—the mother of Paul or the girl who was in love with him—sought to provoke other meetings. Was Mme. Bernardini already nurturing her plan? Was it suggested to her by Laure's marked amiability and the unusual frequency of their encounters?

First, so the story goes, they would greet each other and pass on. Then they got to walking a short distance together. Was Laure hoping to get back to the son through the mother, or did she take pleasure in Mme. Bernardini's company because she was seeking every opportunity to rekindle her suffering?

One day, they were seen going into a pastry shop together. When they came out, Laure was smiling. And Mme. Bernardini seemed less somber, less rigid, than usual.

Laure stopped weeping. She gave the ironmonger's son clearly to understand that he was unwelcome.

She began to dream as she leafed through the catalogues of big Paris stores. She lingered over the bridal gowns.

MME. LAURE has gone up to her room for her siesta. Before she lies down, she opens her desk and removes a large wooden box inlaid with ivory, and a pair of tiny scissors.

She props herself against the pillows. She draws her fringed shawl over her shoulders so that her arms will be free. She opens the box. It contains a large number of photographs taken by whom or where no one any longer knows—old photos, in which the subjects strike affected stances, posing against a leafy background or with a hand resting on the shaft of a broken column.

Mme. Laure examines each picture at length, as if she were trying to remember the time, the place, the circumstances. . . . She selects the photos one by one and brings them up close to her eyes. On the counterpane to her right, she places the photos in which Thérèse appears, full or half length. There are many of these. When the pile seems to her high enough, Mme. Laure begins her work.

With her scissors, she punches a hole in the photo, cuts out a circle here, and oval or irregular rectangle there. She trims, scrapes, scratches, and crops all images of Thérèse. The photos, now pierced by windows or pared along the edges or mutilated by heavy scratches, she replaces in the box according to an order that only she understands. The intact pictures she replaces in a separate tray. She closes the lid of the box.

She stretches out, folds her hands, and begins her nap. In a moment, she is asleep.

Mme. Thérèse has also withdrawn to her room. In front of a rococo dressing table topped by a round mirror, Mme. Thérèse has sat down on a quilted stool. She opens one drawer, then another; on the mahogany tabletop she lines up jars of cream, jars of salve, bottles of perfume, boxes of paste and powder. She leans toward the mirror.

She applies a foundation lotion to her face, then spreads over it a rose cream. Motionless, her face set, she observes the strange mask that stares back at her from the depths of eyes that are of uncertain color, as if drowned in fog.

With the tip of her finger, she scoops up a dab of red cream and applies it to one cheek, then the other. She plasters and powders over wrinkles and the hollows under her eyes. Not a muscle of her face quivers as she contemplates the results of her efforts: the mask is flushed; it is even a glowing red; it avoids age but far from appearing young seems suddenly frozen, ageless. The violent colors make it resemble a death mask. Mme. Thérèse takes up her mascara brush; with a sure hand, she lengthens her eyebrows, thickens them, transforms them into two black crossbeams. With a broad sable-haired brush, she tints her lids blue up to the brows, which she underlines and prolongs toward the temples. She smears her mouth with a shining coat of garnet-red lip rouge.

The task is finished. Mme. Thérèse sits hypnotized by the reflection of a parti-colored face that is hieratic and terrifying, like the visage of a primitive female divinity.

Mme. Thérèse plunges into her reflection; she loses herself, she drowns in it. On the other side of the mirror, the other Thérèse floats under the tarnished glass like a monstrous fish immobilized behind the glass wall of an aquarium. They are two, two women-birds, two women-flowers, women-wyverns, harpies, sphinxes, or dragons, whose befogged eyes, set in carnival faces, are locked each on each.

Then, little by little, the opaque pupils grow moist; fat tears form in the corners of the eyes; contained for an instant by a barrier of eyelashes, they overflow their barrier, and, pouring down, trace black furrows on the painted cheeks. The tears do not dry up; they rush down in cataracts, they inundate the still

69

impassive face and that face on the other side of the mirror.

They mix with the powder, they smear it, they sluice the wrinkles clear, splotch the cheeks, and melt the rouge on lips that gradually begin to tremble.

And suddenly, as if gripped by a cataclysm, the whole face twitches and is convulsed and comes apart: the features dissolve. Mme. Thérèse sobs silently; her shoulders jerk, her bosom heaves and gasps like a pair of old bellows. Blindly she gropes for a big handkerchief, and she sponges, she scrubs, she swabs. From under the diluted mask, the faded skin little by little reappears. Mme. Thérèse becomes herself again, except that her skin is enflamed and her eyes look bruised.

She closes the jars and bottles. She pushes the drawers shut. She throws herself on the bed. Exhausted, she falls asleep.

In a dream, Mme. Laure goes through the motions of cutting, cutting paper with her empty fingers. Mme. Thérèse's breasts rise, and her mouth allows one last hiccuping sob to escape.

In the kitchen, Théodore has just cut some stale crusts of bread into fine pieces. With the crumbs he has set apart, he fashions a short, fat little figure; he shapes it carefully, flattens out a pair of feet, molds two hands; on the top of the head, he plants the brownish tip of a match. With his punk-wicked lighter, he sets fire to the phosphorus, which hisses into flames. Théodore grins as he watches the toupet of Thérèse burn.

The big, peaceful house dozes, abandoned to the heat of a summer afternoon.

70

HAD MME. BERNARDINI been in less hurry to get her son married, the passing of time might have helped her find, eventually, a daughter-in-law worthy of her. But ever since the "tragedy," living alone with her son had been a harassing experience. Paul's trip to Italy had been only a short interlude, and even during it the widow had not lacked worries. She felt at the end of her rope. Perhaps she also feared a sudden turn in fortune for Thérèse. She wanted without delay to place an insuperable barrier between her son and the former milliner. For her, that barrier was marriage.

She found a way to lure young Laure to her house. The girl had just finished her modest studies; with alacrity, she agreed to come twice a week to embroider the Bernardini household linens. If her parents were astonished that she would devote herself to an ancillary task, Laure must have promptly reduced them to silence either by making Father and Mother privy to her plans or by haughtily putting them in their place. Once again, Laure entered the austere mansion by the service door.

Mme. Bernardini gave her very little and only the finest work. On the pretext that her task required good light, she did her stitching and embroidering out on the terrace, where Paul sometimes spent an hour or two in the afternoon.

Was he uncomfortable at meeting the go-between in his ill-fated love affair again? No doubt he avoided her at first, but then, little by little, since she was careful not to remind him by so much as a glance of the mournful past and pretended to have forgotten how brutally he had dismissed her, he got used to her presence.

She herself, since she was swallowing her pride in consenting to see him again, could scarcely have been at ease the first few times. But Laure was pursuing a dream of conquest, of a marriage license. Very likely, she saw herself once again in the guise of a heroine who sacrifices pride to love. The role was to her taste.

When she returned home in the evening, she would look at herself a long time in the mirror, admiring the image she had just offered Paul, for, without vanity, she found herself beautiful. Her sweet, full lips, her long hair, her brilliant eyes, her supple body were so many weapons; she admired their perfection and she maintained them the way a warrior burnishes his sword.

She dressed with such care to go to work at the Bernardinis that even if Berthe had not been informed, she must have guessed Laure's intentions.

Berthe knew about the licentious life into which the Bernardini son had thrown himself. Nonetheless, she let matters run their course, conceiving of no greater happiness for her daughter than for her to join the town's most distinguished family, even if it meant uniting herself with a good-for-nothing.

Laure had abandoned work on her trousseau. She was monograming linens to be added to the fragrant pile that, she hoped, would one day be her own. Berthe supplied her with models of ornamental initials, which she took from long boxes lined with tissue paper. They were brass capitals set in small pieces of delicate wood. Laure rubbed them with chalk before pressing them against the material; a fine blue powder would stick to the tips of her fingers.

For hours on end, Laure embroidered "P"s and "B"s. She interlaced them, surrounded them with crowns, underlined them with knots and bows. Contact with the fabric, although it was the finest linen, would finally irritate her skin. She would lay the work down, rub her pretty hands together, and, laughing, hold them out for Paul to see how she was wearing herself out in his service. He would raise his eyes from *The French Hunter,* shake his head, make some amiable comment, and resume his reading.

Paul had seemed less surly since the young girl was present. His mother, who maintained her unremitting surveillance over him, thought she could detect his recovering a zest for life; she imagined that he seemed brighter on the days when Laure was to come.

As she handled the fine linen sheets, did young Laure think that she would clasp Paul in her arms between their folds? Mme. Bernardini had been either very simple or very astute when she assigned the embroiderer her task.

The happiest time the young people were to spend between those sheets was undoubtedly that summer, when great rectangles of new linen enclosed them in its stiff folds, cascading around Laure's chair and reaching as far as the foot of the armchair where the handsome, indolent Paul coddled his melancholy.

Did he forget Thérèse? He had no occasion to speak of her, and no one knew whether she still occupied his thoughts. He used to tap his leg, grumbling; he insinuated that his wound was the cause of all his woes. Laure would avoid replying; she confined herself to glancing at him with compassion. Since until then he had found few people inclined to pity him, the commiseration of the little seamstress was balm to him.

Sometimes his glance lingered over Laure's well-proportioned bosom, over a leg momentarily revealed, a tight stocking emphasizing the slender calf. When Mme. Bernardini surprised a gleam of desire in his eyes, she was triumphant. Berthe took pains with her daughter's appearance; she advised this or that blouse because its rounded neckline would show her throat to advantage or because the tiny tucks would enhance the line of her bosom.

Thus these two decent, right-thinking mothers worked in

concert to awaken Paul's desire. They would have been shocked had anyone called them procuresses.

Docile, consenting, Laure willingly made herself the bait; Paul became the bream. But they were no longer thinking, neither the one nor the other, of the fisherman's manual.

SUMMER is ending. The days are growing shorter, and the equinoctial winds are bringing the first rains.

Mme. Laure and her callers have retired to the drawing room, where in the evening Théodore lights a blazing fire.

The old women cluster in a semicircle around the hearth; they envelop their legs in worn lap rugs that they call "plaids" —perhaps in memory of long-past travels, outings in horse-drawn carriages, or novels read years ago whose pages were traversed by cavalcades of great lairds sweeping over the heath.

Mme. Laure has a warm drink served. It is Mme. Thérèse who is charged with preparing the lime-blossom or mint tea, with fetching the silver teapot that is kept warm in a padded tea cozy. She arranges the cups, the little spoons, and the sugar bowl on a tray. She handles the tongs with a dexterity born of long practice. She knows the preference of each of the ladies present, and offers them the fragrant drink prepared to the taste of each.

Then, in the half-shadow of the drawing room, where the leaping fire establishes uncertain, shifting borders of a zone of reddish light, nothing is heard for several minutes but the faint sound of lips sipping tea and the tiny clatter of small spoons.

Mme. Constantin says that at the cemetery someone has stolen the marble book on which her dead husband's name and the dates of his birth and death were inscribed.

The younger Mme. Cygne expostulates, are they now going so far as to rob the dead?

75

The elder Mme. Cygne sighs. Times are bad. How is one to adjust to a period that has neither faith nor regard for the law?

Mme. Laure, shuddering, observes that our poor world is headed for destruction. When respect for death vanishes, she says, there is no more hope.

Mlle. du Fleuriel says that such sacrileges deserve the gallows. Mme. Thérèse smiles. For her, she says, the dead are less important than the living.

She arouses a flurry of protest on all sides, but far from being contrite, she confirms her position by an emphatic toss of the head.

Mme. Laure says tartly that Thérèse and her paradoxes have finally managed to astound her. Does Thérèse even know where her own mother's grave is?

Mme. Constantin amplifies; the marble book had cost a mint. Also, the still virgin page had been destined to receive her own dates when she departs—as late as possible—for the beyond.

Mme. Thérèse specifies the site of her mother's grave: at the far end of the left path, third from the wall.

Mlle. du Fleuriel asks thoughtlessly if that is the grave enclosed by a fence where one never sees any flowers.

Mme. Thérèse snorts; when her mother was alive, she detested the scent of flowers. What is the point of giving them to her now? Mme. Constantin observes, with great good sense, that where she is now there is no risk that smells will disturb her.

The younger Mme. Cygne permits an indecorous little laugh to escape, which she quickly smothers behind a lace-framed hand.

Mme. Laure glances severely around the group. Everyone falls silent.

Mme. Constantin finally breaks the silence just as it is threatening to become uncomfortable. She asks why certain people are sensitive to certain smells. For example, she herself has never been able to sniff a violet without suffering violent headaches. Mme. Laure observes that, as far as she is concerned, it is lilac that upsets her.

The younger Mme. Cygne claims that a bouquet of narcissus is enough to make her faint.

Mme. Thérèse says that smells are associated with lost memories; she read so in a newspaper.

Mme. Constantin says that that must be pure foolishness, otherwise she would have to hate all perfumes, her whole life having been nothing but a long train of bad memories.

The elder Mme. Cygne says that new-mown hay brings on her asthma attacks.

Mme. Thérèse claims that asthma is a purely nervous disease.

And Mme. Cygne inquires sharply if Thérèse means to suggest that she is crazy.

The little world clustered about the fireplace becomes agitated, shadows flit over the wall, exclamations explode. It is like a peaceful henhouse after sunset, into which a weasel has just slipped and provoked a cackling emotion amid the rustle of ruffled feelings.

Mme. Laure attempts to restore calm at the cost of an effort that makes the vein in her temple throb and purples her cheeks. She proposes a second cup of lime-blossom tea and motions to Thérèse to serve it. Thérèse rises, obeys wordlessly, and receives some dry, sibilant "Thank you"s, like the pecking of beaks.

Silence falls once more. The roost is again hushed, the elderly hens dream as they revolve their spoons in the warmed porcelain cups.

THE BREAM is said to be a long, flat fish, which is more interesting to catch than to eat, for its flesh proves to be soft and rather tasteless.

This was the case for Paul and Laure.

She succeeded in interesting him, then in attracting him. Urged on by his mother, he married her. And the wedding festivities were no sooner over than the young woman realized that her husband was nothing but an egotistical sensualist, prepared to consider her solely as a carnal diversion.

The wedding night of the romantic Laure cannot have been happy, or her other nights, either, until the onset of pregnancy gave her an excuse to sleep apart. No one followed the young couple on the night of their wedding, and no one even remembers any more where, to conform to custom, they went to hide their honeymoon.

One may surmise it was some country inn not far from town (Madame had already laid out money for the trip to Italy and probably wanted to hold expenses down), a rustic but comfortable establishment, with a large, low-ceilinged bedroom furnished with a great frame bed that was almost invisible under a plump eiderdown quilt. Surely there was also a dark wardrobe, whose cretonne-lined drawers exhaled an odor only of dust and old oak; it had never served any but transient guests and never contained anything but a few clothes stored for a day or two on its shelves.

Perhaps a big mirror hung above the old-fashioned fireplace

of black or gray marble. Young Laure would have looked at herself in it often. It was in that mirror that she cast one last glance after slipping on her embroidered nightgown. Pale with emotion, she was preparing herself to meet a strange and wonderful mystery about which her mother and her books had only half informed her. She smoothed the tucks of the material over her bosom, putting off the moment to call her husband—alone, so she believed, for the last time.

Later, white-faced and haggard, she must have stared into that mirror as if it were stagnant water into which she would have wished to let herself slip, there to die.

In that mirror, she followed, perhaps, the transformations wrought in her by fatigue and disillusionment. Her cheeks grew hollow, her nose pinched, her nostrils white. She passed a weary hand over her forehead, over her bruised eyelids; she slipped a finger between her waist and the band of her skirt, and confirmed that she had lost weight.

The thinness, the pallor, became her, no doubt, and if she went downstairs for meals in the hotel dining room, many admiring eyes must have followed her. She paid no heed. Did she even see the men who bowed as she passed by, and who sometimes stared at her insolently? Despite the—to her, incomprehensible—brutalities that Paul forced her to endure, she loved him, or she thought she loved him, which makes for very little difference.

She was distressed, no doubt, to see that he was apathetic and bored the moment he left their bed. He scarcely spoke, he never took her hands in his, he was interested only in the hunting trophies that hung on the walls, in the heads and antlers of stag, wild boar, and roebuck that were nailed to escutcheons of varnished wood. He ate fast and gluttonously; of the two, it was she, the butcher's daughter, who exhibited the better manners. Furthermore, she was not hungry. A slight, constant nausea gripped her throat; it had seized her the first evening when

Paul, ripping off her nightgown, had virtually raped her. She would nibble at her food, take a sip of wine, and lay down her napkin.

Did they walk after dinner in the garden? There was an arbor, a bench. They sat down. Paul drew arabesques on the ground with the tip of his cane. Laure, chilled, gathered her shawl more closely around her shoulders. They said nothing to each other. After a moment, Paul threw away his cigar. They went back in. It was then that Laure's eyes became fixed, opened wide in fright, in supplication. Paul did not understand their wordless language. She obeyed him.

When, finally, he fell asleep, she got up, repressed the urge to retch, and as she sipped some tepid water, the opaline glass shook in her hand. She wiped her face and body with a damp cloth. She went back to bed. She lay stiffly under the quilt, her eyes open.

She did not weep. She had begun to plunge into a long dream that was not to end; she felt as if she had embarked in a boat that was abandoned to an inexorable current flowing toward a bank she did not know.

When they returned to the big house, the fact that Laure did not look well was ascribed to a happy fatigue. People smiled knowingly, a trifle lewdly. Her cheeks rouged, Laure blinked vacantly.

Thus little Laure had become the wife of Paul Bernardini. What had been at first only a wild dream, a hope, had changed into a goal ardently pursued, and now had become a reality. Laure did not seem happy; she was, nevertheless, established in the big house.

The events that had brought her there did not depend entirely on her own volition, but she had been able to turn them to her own uses. Was it possible that beneath the innocence of a pure and impassioned girl there lurked a measure of guile?

To reconstruct Laure's personality, one relies perforce on

very slender evidence: a few letters, photographs, the gossip of elderly people, tales told at second and third hand. Used in a different way, this same evidence could serve to define a different truth, to trace a different portrait of Laure.

Paul's wealth, his social position—perhaps to the little butcher girl they meant more than the halo crowning her hero. Women who love a warrior see him against a background of combat, and those whose beloved is a sailor do not dissociate him from storms at sea. But when it is a matter of wealth, emotions are no doubt more complex; personal ambition risks becoming fused with passion, even of dominating it or leading it.

Laure had read stories that ended with kings marrying shepherdesses, but perhaps in that happy ending she looked with greater interest at the kingdom than at the Prince Charming. When she used to climb up to the town ramparts to look from a distance at the Bernardini terrace, was it not toward the property that her seemingly devoted love was wafted? Perhaps it was the house, the garden, that made her heart beat faster, rather than the insignificant young man smoking his pipe in the sunlight.

Posterity has preserved only one picture of Paul. It shows him standing in a corner of the big drawing room, one hand resting on a Louis-Philippe pedestal table. No doubt this photo has influenced people's judgments. From the soft line of his chin, from an impression of weakness and self-complacency created by the cast of his features, people deduced a whole personality. Was Paul really the dandy who cared only about himself and his little carnal satisfactions, which is how he is described? A photograph sometimes betrays its subject; too little light, or too much, could have given a questionable cast to a face that did not deserve it; a shadow could have killed the glow in the eyes; the stiff stance imposed by the photographer could have altered the person's real appearance.

That Paul was a sensualist there can be no doubt. But there

is no proof that his appetite for pleasure was the only moving force for the actions of an entire lifetime.

Of Laure, there are hundreds of likenesses. Also, in the Bernardini house one notices a great number of mirrors, not all of which date from the days of the elder Mme. Bernardini. If Laure loved to look at herself so much and to have her image reproduced so often, perhaps it was because a considerable self-esteem, even vanity, made her delight in the admiration of her own person.

Laure's social elevation, her total annexation of the Bernardini house—could they not prove that the young woman coldly decided on the path she intended to follow?

In that case, she would have selected her prey and exploited Paul's simplicity and his appetites to satisfy her ambition.

The one who knew how to play her cards, to steer her bark, could be *not* Thérèse—Thérèse was possibly no more than a pawn on a chessboard—but Laure Bernardini.

Viewed under a different light, the facts assume a different meaning. If one considers the wedding trip of Paul and Laure, one could speculate that it was the young husband who was swindled. Cold and calculating, Laure gave very little to a man who thirsted for love. She was married; the hardest step had been taken; why need she give herself to transports that disgusted her? She refused his hand under the arbor; in bed, she lay frozen; at table, she looked at Paul with repugnance and judged him vulgar, since she prized only the boarding-school manners her mother had taught her to cherish.

When they returned home, Laure's smile veiled, perhaps, an inner satisfaction. She had broken her husband in, granting him only as much as was needed the better to dominate him.

So the story of Paul and Laure could be seen in the light of another lamp, so to speak. Is there ever an end to the deciphering of signs and countersigns?

The whole truth does not exist. Both interpretations of the

facts—the one that makes Laure out a naïve, enamored girl, and the one that depicts her as a calculating climber—can be sustained. It is even probable that both are right, for the emotions of human beings are mixed and their inner motives are often hidden even from themselves.

MME. THÉRÈSE has borrowed Mme. Laure's bowl. She has not had the courtesy to rinse it after using it and to put it back in its place. Therefore, the maid has been searching in vain for the precious receptacle.

Questioned as a last resort, Thérèse says calmly that the bowl is on her dressing table. Mme. Laure flies into a tantrum. At such moments, she resembles an old banging door: without stirring from the spot, she oscillates, she sags, she rights herself, she creaks; her long necklace swings back and forth, her rings jangle against each other, her watch chain gets caught in her cameo pin, and her voice grates like an old lock.

Mme. Thérèse pleads guilty and lowers her head, but inside she is laughing; seen in profile, the hairs on her chin quiver.

She says that she took the bowl to soak her dentures in it.

Mme. Laure asks why Thérèse chose precisely that bowl, and Thérèse replies, simply, because it is the prettiest. Mme. Laure is beside herself. Must one, for such a vile purpose, select a collector's item? That bowl is the last of a set, it is authentic Limoges, it . . . Mme. Laure chokes, she has a coughing fit, she presses one hand to her ailing heart, while Mme. Thérèse wipes away tears that come, perhaps, from suppressed laughter.

The maid goes to Thérèse's bedroom to look for the bowl with the violet pattern. She washes it in scalding water, dries it with care, and replaces it in the sideboard.

Mme. Laure says that she will never again enjoy drinking her coffee from that bowl; it will always seem to her that the porcelain retains a smell, an unpleasant taste.

An unpleasant taste of what, Mme. Thérèse asks.

An unpleasant taste of an old jawbone, of a tooth stump, Mme. Laure says.

Thérèse shrugs and goes out. Mme. Laure swallows a pink pill; little by little, her bosom stops heaving. She shakes her fist in the direction of the door by which Thérèse has left. Her mitten—black against her pale-white skin—makes her hand look like a turkey's claw.

AFTER HER MARRIAGE, Laure led, at least at the beginning, a life quite like her existence as a young girl. Instead of coming only twice a week to the Bernardinis' house, she now lived there. She still embroidered linen with Paul's initials, sitting on the terrace where the pink and blue balls of the hydrangeas were slowly fading.

She seldom saw her parents. They had recently given up their shop, urged to do so by Mme. Bernardini, who disliked having to think that the father of her daughter-in-law was active in the butcher business. Berthe and her husband had retired to their little property, and, having by force of circumstance become rentiers, they now cultivated their untilled land. Since they were never invited to the big house, they began to think that their daughter's marriage had secured few advantages for them apart from the knowledge that they were now connected to the Bernardinis. It was late to have any regrets over the ironmonger's son. Berthe consoled herself by dazzling her acquaintances with tales about the Bernardini splendor. In their household, she asserted, there was not one fork that was not of heavy silver, not one glass that was not of crystal. She spoke of chests overflowing with brocades and laces. She grew lyrical; having seen nothing, she could invent as she pleased.

Eugène was bored. He missed his meat stall and the legs of lamb that he had handled so lovingly for more than twenty years.

They hardly missed their daughter. During the last years, she had become so alien to them that they were rather pleased not to see her any more. She had changed boats, changed worlds,

86

without taking them with her. It was partly their fault. They shrugged. About-face! Such was fate.

Their peaches, now that they were better tended, grew large; their grape harvest was good; their vegetables they sold to shopkeepers in town—and thus, thanks to go-betweens, they remained in trade still. They had adopted a cat and took tranquil pleasure in her company.

When her first child was conceived, Laure did not realize it for some time. In this area she was ignorant, and her mother had not thought—any more than had her mother-in-law—to inform her.

But Mme. Bernardini was keeping watch. Several indispositions, a sallow complexion alerted her. She asked a few questions and summoned the family doctor. Laure learned her great news with no joy.

From one day to the next, she found herself being treated like a precious jewel case enclosing the heir-to-be. She was constrained to give up her needlework; she was enjoined to rise late; the greater part of her afternoons she spent on the terrace doing nothing, jealously watched over, pampered and spoiled, by Madame.

She quickly acquired a taste for this. She also took advantage of her new situation, and begged Paul no longer to disturb her at night. He had to take up quarters in a room adjoining the conjugal bedchamber. Released from her husband's assiduities, Laure began to bloom. As people had attributed her pallor to nights of voluptuous pleasure, they now assigned her flourishing appearance to her pregnancy. And just as she had not denied the first explanation, by her silence she endorsed the second. She began to relish being Paul's wife the moment she stopped belonging to him. An idle life suited her innate indolence. For a part of the day, she went about in her dressing gown. She spent a long time over her toilette; she admired the reflections the silks she wore cast on her skin; she studied her slender

fingers, now no longer irritated by any handiwork; she prome-
naded her nascent plumpness along the garden paths. She felt
like a princess; in imitation of the household, she came to think
of herself as a person of immense importance. She forgot Paul,
and she gave the child scarcely a thought, except when her
mother-in-law joined her. She loved now only herself.

Paul must have felt cheated. Married almost in spite of himself to a young and beautiful girl of whom he had no doubt
hoped a great deal, he found himself bound to a woman of ice.
Now he could not even make use of Laure as an object of
pleasure, which might have contented him; he was forbidden
to approach her. Is this when his thoughts began to turn again
to Thérèse?

Gossip has it that without weighing the consequences she had
left her innkeeper. She was doing housework for several families in town who were not overpunctilious about the morals of
their hired help, and she rounded out her income as best she
could; that is to say, she went with men who were willing to pay
her. Why should she not have been Paul's, if he met the price?

The necklace affair was receding in time. Who knows that it
did not linger in the former milliner's mind as a gratifying
memory? To recall a passion that had brought her lover to the
brink of murder could only flatter her. People have claimed
that toward evening, on the outskirts of town, they used to
come upon the shadows of Paul and Thérèse clasped in embrace. Women were scandalized; men simply laughed. People
felt a modicum of pity for the young wife, but much more for
the mother, who had made the sacrifice of a mésalliance only
to find herself in virtually the same predicament as before.

The Bernardini ladies knew nothing of this. If Paul often took
off, they did not detain him; they were happy to be left alone
to talk of confinements and newborn babies.

It was Mme. du Fleuriel who sounded the alarm. She threw
out hints, she intimated; her words were harmless enough but

her silences spoke volumes. Did she act out of spite? Did she think it only just to aggrieve her old friend, whose son had rejected a flattering offer of alliance with her family and thus left the field open to the man who had recently deserted her daughter? Or was she determined not to be alone in suffering over a child? Unless she sincerely wanted to render a service . . . It is probable that all of these reasons impelled her finally to speak out and, who knows, even to inflict pain in order then to console.

Mme. Bernardini upbraided herself for negligence. She attempted to call her son to account. He simply denied everything.

A young manservant by the name of Théodore had just been engaged. He was a simple fellow who, from the outset, offered Paul Bernardini boundless admiration and devotion. Paul made use of him; he would take him along hunting and talk to him about Thérèse. So, in a way, Théodore possessed Thérèse by proxy. He mentally enjoyed her favors during his stints as lookout when he stood watch by a porte-cochère; and to defend his master's love, which was a little bit also his own, he was ready to swear by all he held holy whatever Paul might ask him to swear.

Thérèse was not satisfied. Paul gave her money, but he wasn't "like a husband," she said. When he was with her, he often looked at his watch; he went home before midnight. Also, she could not believe that Paul forwent dalliance with his wife. She had seen Laure and had been struck by her beauty, and she was jealous of her. Their roles were now reversed. Thérèse took it amiss that Paul should have married and brought a shopkeeper's daughter into his home. In what way was Laure any better than Thérèse? She said she would have countenanced a marriage of convenience with a rich heiress, but she found that an alliance with the daughter of a butcher smacked of a love match.

And the Bernardini house, that great austere establishment

where she would never set foot, became for her a palace out of *The Arabian Nights.*

Paul hoped that Thérèse and Laure would never meet. He knew his mistress was impetuous, and feared she would raise a rumpus. He sought reassurance by telling himself that Laure never left the house.

It is true that she went out seldom. However, she was in the habit of accompanying her mother-in-law to High Mass on Sundays.

One morning, at the end of the service, Thérèse caught sight of the Bernardini ladies on the church steps. She made a scene that no one has forgotten, insulting young Laure, heaping opprobrium on Madame, and spitting on the family tree. Then, laughing until she was breathless, she ran off.

It was to no avail that, later, Paul swore on his honor, lost his temper, reasoned, denied all accusations, begged, promised. . . . That night, Laure had a miscarriage.

Around town, people began to mutter that Thérèse had the evil eye, or that the Bernardini family was under a curse. In the grip of fever, Laure seemed to discover passion and despair once again—unless it was pride that made her agonize and thrash about on her bed as if she had been put to the torch. Madame took drops against apoplexy. Paul consigned Thérèse to the devil and berated Théo, who had encouraged him to go astray. Then, out of all patience, he betook himself to the garden to smoke his pipe. All these females with their tragical moods were beginning to wear him down. To make love to one woman when another denies herself to you—where was the wrong in that? Couldn't one have a wife and a mistress peacefully and at the same time?

He knew many men in town who were living like that, and they seemed none the worse for it.

He summoned Théo, and, pacing together around the circle, they recited, like so many litanies, the charms of the girl lost twice, thrice, lost now perhaps forever. The doctor came out to the garden to say that the young wife was better, that with care, with gentleness . . . And Paul went up to the bedroom to play the tender, attentive husband, whereas what he really longed to do was to bite someone.

BY THE LIGHT of the lamp, Mme. Thérèse is fashioning a velvet rosette for a dress of Mme. Laure's. The younger Mme. Cygne is full of exclamations as she watches those fingers, which have remained agile despite the years. She says that she would love to learn how to make ornaments for her own clothes.

The elder Mme. Cygne grumbles that her sister is talking nonsense. What would she do with a rosette?

She pronounces "ro-*sette,*" in a disdainful tone of voice.

Mme. Constantin says that she has never cared for frills and furbelows. Mme. Laure asks if they are intending to tax her with being frivolous. Mlle. du Fleuriel smiles to herself, her eyes cast down: the rosette reminds her of a dress she once wore, and she describes its bodice decorated with tiny pleats and its skirt scattered with garlands of rosettes. It was a ball gown, a pink ball gown.

Mme. Constantin says that it is hard to imagine Mlle. du Fleuriel in pink. And Mlle. du Fleuriel replies that nonetheless that was the way it was, and that by common consent pink used to be ravishingly becoming to her.

Mme. Thérèse says that it would give her pleasure to teach Mme. Cygne the art of the rosette.

Mme. Constantin is amused: a rosette lesson.

Mlle. du Fleuriel has not emerged from her secret world. Her eyes are still turned inward. She says that she can remember a jewel case her mother had, a solid-silver casket, rectangular, with an engraved lid.

The design showed a shepherd standing behind his shepherdess, who, dressed in a full, beribboned skirt, was trying to blow on a straw. Beneath the engraving, on a banderole, you could read the title of the scene: "The Flute Lesson."

The elder Mme. Cygne says that it is not a question now of flute lessons but of sewing lessons, and that her sister has never been able to learn so much as how to hold a needle.

The younger Mme. Cygne enters a plea. Why shouldn't she try? If she's never finished a piece of handiwork, it's been because whatever was proposed to her was so boring. But this time . . .

Mlle. du Fleuriel says that her mother was fond of the jewel case; she was so fond of it that before she died she asked that it be placed in her coffin.

Mme. Thérèse asks what was in the box, and Mlle. du Fleuriel responds that she never knew.

Mme. Laure suggests that it contained portraits of people dear to her mother. Mlle. du Fleuriel says that in that event she does not understand why her mother made such a mystery about the box.

The younger Mme. Cygne opens her mouth, then blushes and says nothing. Everyone understands that she has just thought something improper. The elder Mme. Cygne is annoyed, but she is unable to refute an unspoken thought; she contents herself with shaking her head violently, like an old horse tossing its head up and down.

Mme. Thérèse clucks softly. Mlle. du Fleuriel exclaims "Oh!" Mme. Constantin grumbles something or other about human frailties being very peculiar indeed.

Mme. Laure observes abruptly that the rain has spoiled the last chrysanthemums of the season.

At which point, Mme. Constantin announces that she has decided to have the marble book replaced on the family grave. But prices have gone up so that she has had to renounce gilt lettering in favor of engraving. She says also—is it not incredible?—that when she was about to supply the information for the inscription, she no longer remembered her dead husband's birth date. As for the date of his death, there was no danger of her forgetting that.

Mme. Laure says that we do not forget the dates of our heavy sorrows.

Mme. Constantin replies that that particular date was rather one of deliverance.

The elder Mme. Cygne says that poor M. Constantin did suffer greatly.

Mme. Constantin affirms that she suffered even more, and longer.

Mme. Laure, wincing slightly, asks Thérèse to bring tea. This evening, it is mint tea. A fresh fragrance rises from the caddy, the aroma of warmed, bruised leaves. It is reminiscent of sweet-smelling herbs trampled underfoot by couples as they stroll under the midday sun. They pause on the far side of a gully running by the road, and as they talk they crush shining tufts of green, alive with tiny winged insects of the same emerald hue; or else they embrace, bruising the mint carpet that serves as their couch and exhales its perfume into the tremulous air.

An entire summer day escapes from the tea caddy. It is as if the walls and draperies of that superannuated drawing room recede, the sofas and the tortuously carved chairs and the dull paintings in their rich frames all vanish. Mournful autumn has fled, and the burdensome years have faded; one would think the laughter of young girls is about to explode, that life is beginning, that old age does not exist.

The elderly ladies no longer speak. They dream, leaving the sugar at the bottom of their teacups to dissolve by itself.

LAURE drank soothing infusions and a decoction called "white potion," good for cleansing the blood and reducing fever. She was better, but she was not walking yet; her feeble legs still could not support her. Helped by Théodore, Paul carried her out onto the pink terrace every day so that she would have a little fresh air. He would sit down beside her and make an effort to talk to her; he tried to be considerate and even asked her permission to light his pipe. Laure must have remembered the hours she had spent on that same terrace as an invalid's companion or a seamstress; now and then, her eyes would fill with tears. Was she thinking of her dead child or the failure of her marriage? She had always been secretive, and she was growing more so.

When her parents came to see her, she had them stay with her only a short time, and dismissed them with the excuse of her fatigue. It seemed clear that she would never be close to them again. Her life was in the big house; she was a Bernardini, and had she not paid dearly enough for it? A kind of affection had developed between her and her mother-in-law, perhaps because they bore a common grief, visited on them by a man whom each in her way loved.

For Laure had begun to love Paul again because Thérèse had taken him away from her. This time her love was rooted in a greater reality, for now Laure was a woman, and although she remained a stranger to carnal pleasures, she knew their nature. She could imagine Paul and Thérèse together; she suffered from a jealousy so intense that at times she believed she would now enjoy experiences that had disgusted and humiliated her.

She used to close her eyes. The soft woolen coverlet pulled up to her chin brushed against her throat. The mildly crisp air caressed her face. She thought of Paul's hands on her. She thought of them with shame, yet a warmth invaded her, and desire swelled her belly, where she felt her blood pulsing as if that were where her heart now dwelled.

These were passing crises; like fever attacks, they did not last long. Yet, in thinking about herself, Laure realized that she was changing.

As for Paul, once again deprived of Thérèse he became aware that his wife glanced at him now and then in a certain way. And, in lieu of anything better, he began to hope for embraces enjoyed in legitimacy.

LAURE'S FATHER was concerned about her loneliness and grief, and, remembering that once upon a time she had seemed to like animals, he offered her a dog.

People have very little to say about Eugène Lambert, the former butcher, because, it seems, there is very little to be said. He appears to have been a peaceable human being who asked nothing of life except work and a little happiness. Had it not been for his ambitious wife, he would have achieved his modest ideal. He had let himself be dragged toward problematical grandeurs out of weakness, no doubt, and perhaps he felt remorseful that he had delivered his only daughter over to Paul Bernardini. Knowing that she was ill and unhappy, he tried to ease her distress.

The dog was a creature of uncertain breed, with short hair of a nondescript brown and tiny, nervous feet that constantly shook. She was given the name of Sadda.

She used to sleep in a basket at Laure's feet, and if her mistress ventured as far as the garden, she would trot along behind her. Sometimes Laure took Sadda on her lap and talked to her gently and stroked her head. But she would soon put the dog down again, disliking her smell, and would bury her nose in her lavender-scented handkerchief.

The idea of a dog pleased Laure, no doubt, but not the reality. She was capable of loving only images that were clean, odorless, savorless. She had been conditioned to detest the vulgar; to admire the beribboned sheep in pastoral poems rather than flocks in pasture; the poor, if decent and grateful; village maidens, if pure and betrothed; flattering portraits of rich, stable families. Blinded by ready-made figurations of reality, she remained separated from life by a sheet of frigid glass.

Accordingly, she did not become attached to her dog. She liked to feel it near her, however, and she fed it, and had it brushed daily by Théodore, who grumbled. He preferred hunting dogs, which had no claim on the amenities of the house. Sadda continued to sleep in Laure's bedroom, in the daintily arranged basket. The dog loved only her mistress, and was jealous of her.

So, when Paul wished to return to the conjugal bed, he ran afoul of the hostility of a snarling little beast that bared its teeth at him.

It was late, and the household had long been asleep. In Laure's bedroom, the night light cast a bluish glow over the sleeping young woman. She awakened with a start when she heard Sadda growl, and she turned on her lamp.

She saw Paul, in nightclothes, furiously brandishing a poker over the dog's head. Sadda's last yelp sounded together with Laure's scream: with one well-aimed blow, Paul had killed the animal. How could Laure have received her husband when the dog's dead body was lying before the fireplace? Did the blood dripping from Sadda's head remind her of other blood, that of her own rape on her wedding night? Half fainting, she pushed her executioner away with a groan. What happened then she cannot have known; seized again by fever, she had sunk into unconsciousness.

It seems that at some point Mme. Laure took to fancying nocturnal walks. If asked why she goes out at night, perhaps she would answer that she prefers to wander in the garden rather than toss and turn in her bed, a prey to what she calls "the wide-awakes."

As soon as everyone is asleep, she slips on her dressing gown, pins a veil over her hair, steps into her slippers, and, despite the chill, goes downstairs. The last leaves are falling from the trees, and the terrace paving is littered with them. There are only clusters of chrysanthemums and marigolds and a few dahlias that the recent rain has not demolished; with corollas bent, they are still standing.

Mme. Laure's footsteps crush the dead leaves with the sound of rustling taffeta. Between the bare branches, the sky seems larger, and the moon rolls across it through avalanches of tormented clouds. Almost always a wind is blowing. It lifts the lapels of her fur-trimmed dressing gown, it refreshes her old face. No doubt it brings—in the perfume of fading flowers and earth and rain water—some recollection of autumns gone by: a cistern, its water tasting of moss, over which one leaned to shout one's name to the echo; gray-and-yellow All Hallows' vacations; visits to the cemetery; walks in the woods, where one searched, vainly but joyously, for chanterelles. . . .

The tour of the circle is soon made. Mme. Laure repeats it once, twice. She dilates her nostrils to sniff the north wind. Her veil floats behind her. She resembles a dark barge slipping along the circular canal of the garden path.

99

When she passes by Théodore's rabbit hutches, Mme. Laure wrinkles her nose. It is true that the smell of the cages is strong, in spite of the care the gardener lavishes on them. Is it the damp air that heightens the odor of dung and makes the straw rot faster?

The big rabbit shifts position and bumps against the wire. Mme. Laure pauses. Absent-mindedly, she slips a finger through the wire net, and then cries out; disturbed in her dreams, the big rabbit has bitten her.

In the dark, Mme. Laure cannot see her wound very well. She brings her hand up closer to her face. The blood is trickling down to he wrist, and disappears under the sleeve of her quilted gown. Mme. Laure moves away quickly; as fast as she can, she runs back to the house, hurries up the steps, then the stairway. As she toils upward, her breath grows shorter. She reaches the landing. A few steps more and she is in her bedroom, where at last she can examine her injury.

The big rabbit has long teeth. The fingertip is bitten through and the blood is still flowing. At the sight, Mme. Laure is assailed by weakness. She rings the bell for Mme. Thérèse, then lies down, her eyes closed, her arm upraised and resting against the headboard of the bed.

Mme. Thérèse arrives. Her face is puffy with sleep, and her eyes squint. She utters little exclamations that whistle between her toothless gums.

She turns the wardrobe upside down searching for linen, de Bully spirits, or she knows not what. She wipes away the blood, asks questions, and flutters helplessly about, while Mme. Laure's cheeks turn paler and paler, revealing beneath the pallid skin a tiny network of acne rosacea.

Mme. Laure has fainted. Thérèse still flutters, scolding, grumbling, sighing, groaning amid the scattered linens, asking the same questions over and over. Why has Mme. Laure got dressed at that hour of the night, what has she done, who has hurt her? Thérèse pours a jug of water over the stricken woman, drenching the bedclothes to no purpose. She has crushed the flagon of spirits, which diffuse an acrid scent throughout the room. She leans over the bloodless face sunk in the creases of the pillow, and, as if seized by a sudden inspiration, she slaps it smartly. Mme. Laure opens her eyes.

With signs, she asks for a pill. She makes an effort to raise herself on the bed, and swallows it. Then she points to her hand, which Thérèse, in her panic over the fainting spell, has forgotten. Mme. Laure has her finger bathed and wrapped. Then, leaning back against the pillow, she stares scornfully at Thérèse. And Thérèse forgets her questions; she seems to grow smaller, more mushy, more shapeless than ever.

With a gesture, Mme. Laure dismisses Thérèse, who withdraws, having elicited not one word of explanation.

LAURE 'S SECOND ILLNESS was brief. Was it really an illness? By general agreement, it was thought that a sensitive creature, already sorely tried, had been laid low for a few days by a simple nervous shock.

It does seem, in fact, that Laure came out of this last illness fortified, liberated forever from her timidity, from her sense of inferiority that made her so diffident when faced by the family she had married into. The fragile, dreamy girl gave way to a woman conscious of her own worth.

People who reminisce about young Laure during the first months of her marriage call her by her first name, but when they are recalling the years that followed on the death of the little dog Sadda, they call her Mme. Laure.

It is possible that Laure's nature did not change but that the incident of the dog led her to reveal in her outward behavior what until then she had kept in the privacy of her heart. A portrait dating from this period shows Laure Bernardini wearing a dress with a large diamond-shape pattern, long full sleeves, and a bodice embellished with a bertha. She is leaning casually against the terrace balustrade. Behind her, the garden, blurred and dense, provides a romantic background. It is a gracious image that time has only slightly faded. If one examines the photo closely, one discovers that the young woman's face has lost its soft imprecision, its childish contours. The chin is firm. The wide-open eyes, set well apart, express a tranquil decisiveness; under the arching brows that separate them from the smooth expanse of the forehead, they are the eyes of an adult, assured, rich in experience.

The fear Paul used to inspire in Laure must by that time have changed into scorn.

One finds no further trace of quarrels, scandals, or jealousy in the annals of the Bernardini family. And yet Paul had just resumed his relationship with his former mistress once again.

Thérèse, who had journeyed from bed to bed, and whose merits were toasted nightly around the billiard tables at the Grand Café, had only had to make a single sign to win Paul back. If she refused to grant him an exclusive claim on her charms, she did give him preferential status, no doubt by right of seniority.

Again Paul prolonged his evenings away from home. From time to time, however, he visited his wife still. She did not repulse him. She found his breath winy and his ways rough, as usual. Sometimes he hurt her, and she would bit her lips to keep from crying out, for fear, perhaps, that he would mistake it for a groan of pleasure. She waited patiently for her husband's transports to end, then turned on her side and went to sleep, conscious of a duty done.

Because of her partner's clumsiness and his coarseness, and perhaps also because of her own inability to give herself, she had grown definitely unresponsive to the love of a man.

Come spring, in the garden now pink with roses, Laure began to take slow, thoughtful walks. She was pregnant again. It was no doubt what she had wanted.

This time, she must have determined to bring her pregnancy to term, to minimize incidents that might upset her. Now turned inward, she no longer thought of herself as the seat of a physical phenomenon that was independent of her own will, as the passive instrument needed to continue a family line. She was Laure Bernardini, and she was beginning to build her own child.

She took a smaller part in conversations. Her needle moved

in and out of pieces of fine batiste, but her glance wandered toward the clumps of flowering shrubbery or followed the flight of the swallows. Had someone told her she must look at beautiful things in order to have a beautiful child, and did she believe that?

Now and then, she would gently stroke her belly under her gown. She responded to questions in monosyllables. And if someone mentioned to her that her silences were long indeed, she smiled.

In the evening, when Paul would get up from the table, throw down his napkin, and pretend he was going out to join his friends at the Grand Café, only his mother looked at him in anguish. Laure seemed not even to see him.

The maid would clear the table. Madame and her daughter-in-law would retire to the drawing room. Both would sew, or read, until the moment when each rose and carried off her lamp.

Paul came home later and later. Since he was sleeping again in the room that adjoined the conjugal bedchamber, Laure hardly heard him. Was he still part of the house? Nothing was asked of him any more. The rule of the women was definitely established in the family. Any man but Paul might have been affected by this, and perhaps might have attempted to react. But he reveled in his regained freedom without thinking about the price he had paid for it. He took no pains to conceal his meetings with Thérèse; sometimes he took her hunting with him. Théo accompanied them; from a distance, he heard their laughter as they rolled together among the ferns.

The tenant farmers were aware of their master's adventures, and joked about him among themselves. It was he they judged ridiculous, not his wife; she—she had a right to their respect, she was a "lady" who knew how to comport herself.

Laure, her pregnancy conspiring, assumed a more and more imposing carriage, a noble bearing; to her, people bowed low.

Laure's first son came into the world at chrysanthemum time.

He was handsome and strong. Proud of having a son and, no doubt, ever so slightly repentant, Paul abandoned Thérèse for the duration of a week. But since no one took any notice of his belated solicitude, he promptly resumed his old way of life.

THE BANDAGE that Mme. Thérèse has carefully constructed for Mme. Laure's finger does not fail to arouse the ladies' curiosity. Mme. Laure pretends that the bandage conceals a scratch. Mme. Constantin says that little hurts must not be neglected; she has seen mere rose pricks become infected.

The elder Mme. Cygne, who served briefly as a volunteer nurse, asks to see the wound. The younger Mme. Cygne vouches for the fact that her sister has a gentle touch.

Mme. Laure gives signs of impatience.

With authority, the elder Mme. Cygne takes her arm, immobilizes it, and begins to unroll the gauze bandage, while Mme. Thérèse watches with a crafty eye.

On the swollen, bluish flesh the traces of a bite are so apparent that all the ladies cry out. And Mme. Laure is obliged to relate the story of the rabbit.

The elder Mme. Cygne affirms that animal bites can lead to serious consequences.

The younger Mme. Cygne, shivering, speaks of tetanus, and Mlle. du Fleuriel dares to pronounce the word "gangrene."

The moment these words are uttered, they expand menacingly and people the drawing room with terrifying shadows.

Mme. Laure tries clumsily to rebandage her finger, but she is trembling. Mme. Thérèse seems to defer the moment of coming to her aid.

Advice explodes on all sides. Mme. Constantin advocates soaking in salt water—coarse salt, that goes without saying. The elder Mme. Cygne risks modern terminology and speaks of antibiotics. The younger Mme. Cygne cites penicillin, then falls silent, embarrassed to have trespassed on her sister's domain.

Mme. Thérèse has—finally—seized the ailing finger, and is swaddling it as she would have done with an infant, all the while asking aloud how it was that Mme. Laure could have let herself be bitten.

Mme. Laure says that she merely brushed her hand over the wire. The rabbit was sleeping, no doubt; when it was awakened suddenly, it must have been frightened.

Mme. Thérèse says that rabbits are rather gentle-natured. She adds that in broad daylight Mme. Laure would have run no danger. The younger Mme. Cygne exclaims, "It was at night, then?"

It was at night, Mme. Laure confirms. Confronted by the astounded faces of her companions, she becomes annoyed. Does one not have the right to walk at night in one's own garden?

Soothingly, Mme. Constantin recalls Mme. Laure's well-known bouts of insomnia. Mme. Thérèse sighs; how many years it's been that Mme. Laure hasn't slept. She herself sleeps like a top, but sometimes she is roused by the tinkling of a spoon against a cup, by sighs, by the dry cough she knows so well: insomnia, discomfort, warm tea, and sulfur pills from Bagnères-de-Luchon. . . .

Ordinarily, Mme. Thérèse does not speak at such length. They all look at her. Animation has flushed her cheeks, her wig has slipped more markedly askew; one would think she is setting out to do battle. But Mme. Laure's commanding eye holds her in thrall, and little by little Mme. Thérèse loses her bellicose air; she lowers her head.

The conversation resumes more calmly. After considering various types of wounds, and the treatments to be applied, the ladies move on to vicious animals. Mme. Constantin speaks of a horse of her late husband's that used to let fly with cruel kicks and that ended up at the knacker's.

The younger Mme. Cygne tells the horrible story of a cat that ate its own kittens.

Mlle. du Fleuriel recalls a canary that used to peck its cage companions to death.

Mme. Laure speaks of her little bitch Sadda, who was jealous. The younger Mme. Cygne inquires what became of her, and Mme. Laure replies that she had to be put away.

Mme. Thérèse says that she has heard this story a hundred times, and she is about to retell it when Mme. Laure cuts her off by ordering her to put a log on the fire.

WHEN ONE MENTIONS the period that separates the birth of Laure's first son and the death of her mother-in-law, little information is forthcoming. It seems that, strengthened by her new experience, the young woman shook off the Bernardini yoke entirely. People say that she brought the child up according to her own lights, rejecting most of the old wives' counsel and the wet-nurse tricks of the trade that were showered on her. It seems that she went so far as to forbid visitors to kiss her son on the face.

People say also that around this time Paul stopped frequenting Thérèse. Had his wife taken him to task? Perhaps she was already thinking ahead to little Jacques's adolescence and feared the effects of a bad example? She had grown fiercely attached to the child; one can even surmise that it was the first love of her life that was not a self-seeking quest. However, people also relate that Thérèse had left town around that time, taking off with some philanderer or other who promised her money and happiness. A reconciliation must have taken place between Laure and her husband, in consequence of which the young woman was to bear a second child. The months passed. Grown stout and heavy, a happy mother surrounded by respect, Laure no longer bore any resemblance to the young girl of before. She helped Mme. Bernardini receive in the solemn old drawing room, and she was not afraid to assert herself.

On her advice, Paul had begun to busy himself with his properties. He made out fairly well, provided that his wife kept the books. He bounced his son on his knee, let the child seize his beautiful pipe, and laughed, together with his wife, at the little boy's grimaces.

The big house had come to life again, and for this everyone —her mother-in-law the first—thanked Laure.

People relate that the baptism of Laure's second child was surrounded by great pomp. Older relatives had stopped being cool, and they were invited in droves. Relatives came from all parts of the country. Of the newborn son, one saw little more than a small red face, but people exclaimed over his beauty; silver mugs, monogramed coverlets, egg cups, and napkin rings showered around him. Laure, who had wanted a girl, gracefully accepted the congratulations offered her. Two sons had been born to her, two males who would insure the descent in manly fashion; the family name would not disappear, the family estates would have masters.

In the midst of the general rejoicing and while glasses of champagne were being tossed off, Mme. Bernardini suddenly felt faint, lay down on a settee, and departed this life. She still had, so say the gossips, the taste of champagne on her tongue; she must have died of joy.

The burial followed directly on the baptism. Flowers that people had sent to the infant served to embellish the last abode of the grandmother. That is why Mme. Bernardini, who was abandoning this world at a suitably ripe age, departed for the cemetery followed by a wake of white roses and lilies.

Once the old lady was buried, one can imagine that Laure made a reckoning, that she drew up a kind of life balance sheet. She found herself mistress of the big house, of fields, woodlands, farms, and hamlets. Paul seemed submissive. She was twice a mother. Now plump and full-blown, she took the measure of her importance, her dignity. The keys to the house cupboards, which now the maid returned to her custody, did not repose on a velvet cushion, but they symbolized her status: she was queen.

MME. LAURE studies her swollen hand. Mme. Thérèse, as she bandages it, is not sparing of comments likely to sow concern. Has Mme. Laure noticed the red streak on the forearm, visible below the sleeve of her jacket? Mme. Laure sees nothing, but Thérèse insists that she clearly discerns an inflamed line running from the wrist to the bend of the elbow; it is a sign that the infection is spreading. Mme. Laure feels no pain in the armpit? Mme. Laure presses the designated spot at length. At first, she feels nothing but, by dint of pinching the flesh in search of a ganglion, she provokes an irritation that troubles, then frightens her. Thérèse is ordered to have the doctor come posthaste.

While waiting for the doctor, Mme. Laure has her hand soaked in a basin of water and chlorine. She looks through the foul-smelling liquid at her poor, injured hand, which, with the fingers spread wide, resembles a sick starfish. Shrilly, she bewails the thoughtlessness that made her stick her index finger in the rabbit's cage.

In a spiteful tone, as she brushes Mme. Laure's hair, Mme. Thérèse says that anyone who walks outdoors at night exposes himself to some danger. While talking, she jerks on a rebellious lock of hair, and Mme. Laure, instead of responding, groans and looks up at Thérèse beseechingly. Thérèse turns gentle; hair by hair, she untangles the knot, she caresses and soothes the old head delivered into her care. Having sown panic, she now undertakes to reassure: the doctor is going to come; soon it will all be just a bad dream.

Stripped of her habitual hauteur, Mme. Laure says that she is afraid of being sick, and that she has a horrible dread of dying. Mme. Thérèse says that no matter how one cuts it, death could not be far off for both of them. They have a long life behind them; their old age is passing peacefully, in comfort and in friendship. What have they to complain of? Mme. Laure says that without complaining one can still be afraid to die.

Mme. Thérèse says that life is like a long walk one takes along a road bordered by empty coffins. The advancing cohort, numerous at the outset, diminishes as its members—without order of age, for that matter—lie down, one after another, in the waiting coffins. Each person knows that his is there, somewhere, by the side of the road. It's better not to think too much about it.

Mme. Laure shivers. She says that she tries to believe in the life everlasting, but she wonders what will become of them. Have they led a good or a bad life?

Mme. Thérèse says that, as far as that's concerned, she does not worry about it much. Through all the years, a person has to defend herself, all unarmed against so many snares and traps. . . . A person lives as best she can. Everybody gets along in her own fashion. There is no good or bad. Mme. Laure's tears are brimming. She searches for a handkerchief and dries her eyes.

Mme. Thérèse has picked up the hairpins; she holds them between her teeth. She braids the white locks, and her hand is gentle as it brushes the temples, rolls and twists the tresses, and arranges them in a chignon. She says that the doctor will be there any minute. With her sound hand, Mme. Laure grasps the arm of Thérèse, who murmurs to her tenderly and comforts her like a child.

IT WAS FUTILE for the town to hold itself aloof from the affairs of the world and to attach more importance to small local scandals than to international quarrels: the war touched it nonetheless. Many men had to go off to fight without having time to ask themselves if the game was worth the candle. Paul Bernardini was one of them.

Little is known about Paul's war years. He very likely suffered, as did others. He was neither killed nor wounded nor crowned with glory.

In her husband's absence, Laure had to manage her family and its possessions alone. Her authority increased accordingly. Her sons were growing up, they respected her as the supreme power in their lives, and no doubt she would never have stopped ruling as the absolute mistress of her domain had it not been for the Spanish flu.

As some people recall it, Thérèse and the flu arrived in town together. Others say that the flu preceded Thérèse. What is certain is that the flu and Thérèse came from the same city, the one to which the young woman had gone in the wake of a fun-loving wine salesman. The salesman had just died at the front, and Thérèse, who had waited for him more or less prudently in the hope of marrying him (she was not getting any younger and was beginning to worry about her future), found herself in the same situation as before.

She came back to the town of her birth out of habit or lassitude, or because that was her destiny.

At the same time, the epidemic, which had started to invade

113

the town, spread rapidly. The first to be struck down was Mlle. du Fleuriel; others followed; many died. The doctors, over-worked and discouraged, were saying that the flu was actually the plague, thereby helping to aggravate public turmoil.

Measures were taken to keep track of the dead. They had to be buried immediately not only to prevent contagion but also because rumor was rife that they turned completely black in the blink of an eye, which people accustomed to pale cadavers found terrifying.

Cresylic acid was poured into sewers and gutters, and the powerful smell of the disinfectant wafted from the town toward the surrounding fields. People acquired the habit of eating nothing that was not cooked and cooked again. They disciplined themselves to stop shaking hands with their best friends, even though it might cause hurt feelings, for fear that they might be germ-carriers. They barricaded themselves in their homes.

Laure had first decided to entrust her sons to her mother, thinking that in this way she would be removing them from the path of the epidemic, since her mother still lived outside the town walls. She had to abandon the idea: Berthe, struck down herself, died in a short time, followed soon after by her husband. Laure had no recourse other than to burn fragrant herbs in every available receptacle, confine her sons to their bedroom, and wash every object she used in chlorinated water.

The maid fell ill in her turn, then the two boys, then Théo-dore. Terrified, Laure went from room to room to tend them all, and implored the doctor to save her children.

One imagines her wandering about the house, the air heavy with fumes from the pots, she tottering with anguish and fa-tigue, telling herself a hundred times over that she would will-ingly lose everything she possessed for the sake of her sons' health.

She would drop into a chair, cross her hands on her knees, and doze off, only to jump up, thinking she had heard a call, and as

114

she hurried upstairs again, she would wonder what she was about to find, whether it would be the end.

It seemed that the children would pull through, but the maid was worse. Laure was alone to do all the work, provide all the care. There was not a single woman in town who would have been willing to come to work in the house.

So, at least, Laure thought. She was mistaken; there was Thérèse.

Alerted by rumors about town, no doubt, Thérèse dared to knock at the door and, lowering her eyes before Laure's stunned expression, she offered her services, insisting that the danger of contagion did not frighten her.

Laure was far from feeling any bitterness, any jealousy. The war, then the flu, had altered values and uprooted set ideas. Young Mme. Bernardini was aware that at her back was a dwelling inhabited by invalids and invaded by immense disorder. She herself could scarcely keep on her feet, and a hundred times had asked herself what would happen to her children if she herself succumbed. This being the case, she took what she found at hand. She stepped aside. Thérèse entered the house.

She was never to leave it.

THE DOCTOR gave Mme. Laure an injection. He ordered several medicines and disinfecting salves. He scolded the invalid. What was she thinking of, getting herself bitten by a rabbit?

Mme. Laure, plaintive but reassured, reigns again in her drawing room, among her good friends who condole, cajole, and recount endless stories of their own misadventures, the accidents of each and every one of their relatives, and the mishaps of their acquaintances. Mme. Thérèse is silent. She serves the medicinal infusions; she does not forget the time for the pills. A slight smile brushes her lips when she leans attentively toward her mistress, the glass of medicine in her hand.

When the ladies have gone, Mme. Thérèse helps Mme. Laure to bed. The poor woman is much hindered by having to carry her arm in a sling. Thérèse turns down the bed, smooths the sheets, plumps the pillows. Then, when Mme. Laure is stretched out, Thérèse sits down by the head of the bed and the two chat a moment longer.

Mme. Thérèse says that Mme. Laure has had a lucky escape. She dares speak out now, but before she had thought all was lost.

Mme. Laure says that Thérèse is exaggerating. It was only a very little bite.

Mme. Thérèse says that the rabbit could have been mad.

Mme. Laure would like to know how an animal locked up in a cage could get rabies.

Mme. Thérèse says that such things have been known to happen.

116

Mme. Laure suppresses a shiver. She says that she is glad to have come out of it so well.

Mme. Thérèse asks what Mme. Laure has decided about the rabbit. Mme. Laure is surprised. What should she have decided? The animal had acted within its rights. It was she who had been foolish to awaken it.

Mme. Thérèse says that since the fatal night she has not been able to sleep. She has the constant impression that she hears Mme. Laure going out into the garden to get herself bitten.

Mme. Laure insists that she will not be caught that way again.

Mme. Thérèse says that in this she recognizes her mistress's unfailingly kind heart. Then she falls silent and shakes her head until Mme. Laure asks her what she is thinking.

Mme. Thérèse says that if it were up to her, she would not let the animal live.

Mme. Laure, appalled, asks if Thérèse would have the rabbit killed. And Mme. Thérèse replies that she would sacrifice it without a moment's hesitation.

Mme. Laure says that Théodore would be upset. And Mme. Thérèse says pfft . . . one hand raised, the thumb brushing the other fingers.

Mme. Laure says that, all the same . . .

And Mme. Thérèse says that this decision is not for her to make, that she has said nothing, absolutely nothing. She gets up, puts the chair in its place, lights the night lamp, and withdraws on tiptoe.

THÉRÈSE seemed to take her task to heart. She, the disorderly, the harum-scarum, made a great effort to put the big house back to rights. She proved gentle with the children, patient with their whims, and inventive in amusing them. They began to love her.

To Laure it must have seemed that the Thérèse who busied herself with her children was not the same person whose evil spells she had once feared—when she took the time to think about it at all, which was seldom. The old servant was dying, and Théodore was getting no better. Laure herself began to have chills, and she fought as best she could to hold out against illness. But fatigue had made her an easy prey; she finally collapsed, unconscious, on the stairs.

It was Thérèse who carried her to her bed.

Laure suffered from exhausting spasms of nausea. Thérèse held the basin, without apparent disgust, when she vomited. She was tortured by headaches, which only Thérèse was able to relieve by tirelessly massaging her neck at the hairline. Where had Thérèse learned to be helpful and efficient? Did her devotion derive from gratitude? She knew that Laure had not welcomed her with a happy heart, that she had taken her in for lack of anything better. She was not acting in memory of Paul, her lover of other days who so often had abandoned her and then picked her up again, and for whom she probably nursed feelings of bitterness rather than friendship. Did she wish to make herself indispensable so as to insure herself an honorable refuge, with all dark shadows lifted?

She had never seemed to be a calculating person, but perhaps, having frittered away her youth, she was finally worried about the years ahead.

The truth of it is, it seems that Thérèse had become attached to Laure. Given to swift changes of feeling and to caprices, she could suddenly have felt pity, even tenderness, for the young woman who had struggled so valiantly before falling ill, who was still fighting despite the fact that fever plunged her into almost continual unconsciousness. Perhaps in Laure she recognized a woman of her own stature, far superior to weak Paul.

One can wonder also whether the beauty of Laure, now plump and in full bloom, had not moved her. In those days, when opulent women passed for being "beautiful" women, Laure must not have lacked charms. Below a waist that had remained slender, her hips, they say, had a royal amplitude. She had kept her pale complexion, her soft creamy skin, and the delicate gold chain that encircled her throat accented its roundness. People vouch for her having a high-arched, slender foot and a well-turned ankle. Beneath her jacket, her breasts were still firm; one imagines them marbled, delicately veined with mauve, and stained with large brown aureoles.

Laure recovered.

The flu, for that matter, seemed to be beating a retreat.

The war was over, and the townspeople, who had been more sorely tried by the flu invasion than by the outcome of battles, rejoiced more over the end of the epidemic than over what was then termed "our victorious arms."

Paul Bernardini returned, unscathed and equipped with a black beard. Finding Thérèse installed in his own home, he was wordless with astonishment. But she so little resembled the virago of his wild-oats years that presently he became accustomed to her presence and looked on her as an ordinary servant.

The old servant was dead. Théo was beginning to mend, and the children, both recovered, played in the garden, where a

119

golden autumn trailed mists layered by the rays of the sun. The house was peaceful. Thérèse's eyelids were stained blue by weariness, but she bustled about the vast rooms, efficient, sure of herself and of her competence.

Several women presented themselves at the big house hoping to be engaged as maid. Laure thanked them; she was keeping Thérèse.

Was it Laure's idea to have Théodore and Thérèse marry? That is what wagging tongues said at the time. With flu and war forgotten, the townspeople were reverting to their favorite pastimes of malicious gossip and meddling. Once again, they began to whisper and vilify; they spoke ill of both Paul and Thérèse. The old scandal was not so far in the past for righteous souls not to dredge it up from oblivion. Well-meaning persons (one could not doubt their intentions) went about repeating that Paul and Thérèse were achieving their ends: the trollop was installed in the very house, and old Mme. Bernardini must be turning in her grave.

The Cygne ladies no longer dared call on Laure for fear they would be shown in by Thérèse. Mlle. du Fleuriel sedulously kept her eyes lowered for fear of catching a glimpse of the loose woman. They did not dare speak out. Laure would have answered, rightly enough, that when she needed help she had waited for them in vain. Mme. Constantin came straight to the point: Laure should get rid of Thérèse. It was then that the masters of the big house conceived of a way around the issue, and Paul proposed the deal to Théo. Théo did not hesitate long. The material advantages seemed to him considerable; also, in his simplicity, perhaps he imagined that in a measure Thérèse would belong to him; he had dreamed of that so often in the days when he used to roam the woods with his master.

The marriage took place.

Thérèse profited thereby, without doubt, and Théo's disappointments befell him only later.

Tongues stopped wagging. Since appearances had been

saved, the Bernardini house had once again recovered its good name; Thérèse was a maid, pure and simple, like any other; Laure was employing a married couple as her servants. The matter was closed, the scandal smothered. Despite recent upheavals in the world at large, for the town, marriage continued to be the panacea, the guarantee of surface respectability. And if, by chance, Paul lapsed into his old ways again, people would close their eyes to what would then be nothing more—Thérèse being no longer a prostitute—than a banal affair with a servant.

One imagines that Laure must have given much thought to the matter before stubbornly retaining her former rival in her own house. No doubt she believed she was strong enough to keep the situation in hand. Also, she thought that Thérèse had settled down and that she was devoted to her personally. Lastly, Thérèse had done so much, and in such painful circumstances, that Laure could not help but feel indebted to her. Still other, and more secret motives perhaps pushed young Mme. Bernardini into keeping Thérèse in her service. Could she do without the long sessions of massage that relaxed her every evening? Thérèse's hands were gentle as they brushed lightly over her skin, lingered over the hollow of her throat, and kneaded her back, which ever since her illness had caused her discomfort.

Thérèse dressed Laure's hair and, by unspoken agreement, the two women wantonly prolonged these hairdressing sessions. Laure's brutal husband had botched her initiation into carnal pleasure, but she was sensitive nonetheless to certain contacts that were all the more disturbing for seeming innocent: she loved to have her scalp slowly scratched; under Thérèse's pointed fingers, she was swept by delicious tremors. Those same fingers could draw groans of sensual delight from her as they massaged her smooth, plump back. She used to hold out her hands. Thérèse would massage them between her thumb and index finger, moving up toward the wrist with light circular pressures that sent waves of sweetness rippling through Laure's whole body.

Administered by less expert hands, these ministrations would have been only tiresome. Thérèse turned them into skillful caresses; slowly, she brought Laure under the spell of her magic, preparing her, perhaps, for still other sport. And one can understand how the young woman—who felt revulsion at the touch of a man, having known only Paul's roughness—may have surrendered to the artifices of Thérèse. Her self-love was great; embraced by a like creature, she could imagine herself quivering against another self.

One dares not go so far as to say that Laure and Thérèse were lovers; no one could assert that. But they did live together like two female cats rubbing voluptuously against each other, and the company of the other had become indispensable to each.

OLD THÉO mounts guard near his rabbits. He has set a bag of crusts down beside him, and one by one he passes them through the wire netting. The iron chair that he has dragged up to the hutches rasps with each move he makes. He mutters to himself.

He says that the big rabbit is not vicious. Mme. Laure was very wrong to have frightened her.

He says that all old women are crazy. Isn't it crazy to go wandering around a garden at night?

He says that Mme. Laure got into the habit of walking in the dark back in the days when Thérèse, installed in the house, had taken up again with M. Paul.

He says that Mme. Laure has always been a light sleeper.

He says that even if he had really been the husband of Thérèse, he could not have prevented the thing from happening. It would have called for courage and, he had to admit it, courage was something he had always lacked.

He says that M. Paul did right to get out. Rather than to see what's going on now—a rabbit being accused of murder—a person would better be dead and buried.

He says that he is old and alone.

He says that he is nothing but an old animal that has outlived its day, a broken-down horse, a blind dog, a deaf cat, an ailing billy goat.

He says that if he thinks of his youth he believes he is remembering someone else.

He says that there is a time for everything, even a time to die.

PAUL probably guessed nothing about the subtle bonds that united Thérèse and Laure. It was not that he was urged on by jealousy when, one evening, he climbed up to the new servant's bedroom.

Did Thérèse think that she was betraying Laure—a double betrayal, perhaps? Did she receive Paul with weariness, with resignation, or with joy? Perhaps she surrendered her body, attaching no importance to the act since she had performed it so often. One could not say, any more than one can analyze with certainty Laure's reactions when she discovered the lovers' maneuver.

Laure slept lightly, like every mother conditioned to hear the slightest call from her children. Detecting the sound of Paul's slippers as he returned to his room, she quickly understood.

By keeping Thérèse in her house, she had behaved in such a fashion that this consequence could not fail to develop. One even wonders whether, unconsciously, she had not wanted it.

Did she wish to punish herself for loving Thérèse too much? Did she hope to put her friend's fidelity to the test? Or did pride require her to debase two people who still had some ascendancy over her?

More plausibly, Laure had not believed a fresh reconciliation between Paul and Thérèse possible. The one she judged submissive to her will, the other too cowardly to dare profane his own home.

One is amazed that Laure kept silent. She could have enjoined Paul to break off his reprehensible adultery; she could have thrown Thérèse out. She did nothing, and it is in relation to this strange attitude that one loses oneself in conjectures and that Laure's character once again becomes intriguing.

Mme. Bernardini's insomnia dates from this period. The moment she was in bed, in her mind's eye she must have seen her husband in Thérèse's arms, and she could no longer give in to sleep. For all that she was awake, she was not changing the course of events. Nonetheless, it must have seemed to her that were she to fall asleep for an instant she would in some way have deserted her post. She remained on watch and dozed off only in the early-morning hours, after she had heard Paul return to his room.

She continued to abandon herself to the gentle hands of Thérèse. She had herself massaged and coiffed.

The coiffure sessions took place in the bedroom that Mme. Laure still occupies. They unfolded then just about as they do today. Seated on a low chair, an embroidered linen cape over her shoulders, Laure would surrender her long, unbound hair to her maid. She would complain hypocritically about how heavy her hair was, knowing that Thérèse, who even then had to plump out her own chignon with false hair, envied her that opulent mane. Thérèse entered into the game, and exclaimed over the magnificence of the silken tresses she was rolling round her fingers. The séance would go on and on. Neither Thérèse nor Laure wished to shorten it. When, finally, Laure was ready, she would dismiss Thérèse with abrupt coldness.

Order reigned in the house. Copper utensils and silverware shone, windows sparkled, gleaming furniture reflected the light that entered through tall windows barely greened by the shimmer of the trees in the garden. Cupboards filled with neatly arranged linens exhaled a perfume of iris and lavender. From the kitchen came the aromas of slowly simmering sauces.

Laure had engaged a cook and, more and more, she held

Thérèse at her beck and call, having given her the title of lady's companion.

The Bernardinis' acquaintances praised Laure's housewifely accomplishments, compared her to the virtuous woman in Proverbs, and judged her in every respect worthy of her mother-in-law, whom, for that matter, she was coming to resemble physically.

Laure occupied herself only with her children. She was strict with them and watched over the progress of their studies. She wanted them to have brilliant futures, extolled the advantages of professional careers, and refused to see them satisfied to have been born rich, as their father had been before them.

As soon as they were old enough, she sent them to a secondary school in the neighboring city, esteeming the local institution inadequate for them.

With the children gone—and what anguish Laure must have felt to see them leave—the vast house seemed plunged into an almost funereal calm, disturbed only by occasional visitors: one or two couples who were family friends, now and then relatives passing through town. And, every evening, several women who were Laure's contemporaries, the daughters of childhood friends of the old Mme. Bernardini: Mlle. du Fleuriel was even then the unconsoled virgin with the lace collar above her gaunt bosom; the Mmes. Cygne, whose husbands were still living and who were—or believed they were—happily married, threw commiserating glances at Mme. Constantin, of whose conjugal calamities everyone knew.

In the end, Thérèse had been accepted, imposed on the group by her mistress; she sat on a footstool, a little bit apart, and embroidered and never raised her voice.

The children came home for vacations. They showed their mother obedience and respect but little tenderness, since she herself was quite undemonstrative; they ignored their father, who had never managed to become interested in them. They

126

lavished tokens of affection on Thérèse, rigging her out with pet names, and tagging along behind her to her room, to be shown her few little treasures: a barometer in the form of a cottage with two matching doors, from which issued, depending on the weather, a woman with a parasol or a jolly man with an umbrella; a candy box made of shells, the souvenir of some former summer season, which bore the name of a seaside resort in italic script; and, the acme of happy bad taste, a tiny porcelain chamber pot with a blue eye painted on the bottom.

Laure disapproved of her sons' forays into "Auntie's" bedroom, but no doubt she did not find any serious reason to forbid them. The boys would have been surprised. Was Thérèse not their second mother? They used to say this innocently. Thérèse would lower her eyes to conceal her joy. Laure's lips would tighten.

When the children returned to school, the old house seemed emptier than ever. For the first few days, Laure would fall into a kind of apathy, and her friends chided her. Did she not have her husband, her house? Did she not know that to bring children into the world means condemning oneself to someday being abandoned?

With autumn, the hunting season arrived. Paul went out early, followed by Théodore, and came home at the end of the day, smelling of bruised bracken and damp earth. He would exhibit a hare, a few pheasants, or, if he had joined a beat that day, a bloody quarter of wild boar. Laure could not endure the sight or the smell of that dark, feral flesh; she had it quickly borne off to the kitchen, buried her nose in her handkerchief, and provoked guffaws from her husband, who could not understand such delicacy.

127

PAUL used to hang his gun in the vestibule before going to take off his boots and make himself comfortable. The gun seemed to fascinate Laure. She would look at it every time she passed it, and even appeared to make up reasons for crossing the vestibule. Sometimes she went so far as to place her finger on the stock and caress the carvings that embellished it: the head of an old boar with an exaggeratedly long snout, whose tuft of hair continued the design engraved on the metal fittings of the trigger guard. Paul had caught his wife out in her little maneuver, and one day he explained the handling of the weapon to her. She listened attentively for a moment; then, with what seemed to be disdain, she said that that instrument of death did not interest her.

It was perhaps true. But Laure forgot no part of the lesson the evening she took down the rifle and loaded it before climbing the stairs that led to Paul's bedroom.

Here one moves out onto shifting ground. The few rumors, quickly suppressed, on which one could base any claim that Mme. Laure killed her husband, are scarcely more substantial than smoke.

One can imagine that Laure, wearying of the ignominious situation she was supposed to be unaware of, decided one night to end it by a murder.

Why that night and not another? Laure had put up with the intimacy between Paul and Thérèse for years. She had refused to break it up, as another woman would have done, by throwing her rival out. And, since she feared scandal, in killing Paul did she not run the risk of provoking a still greater one?

Unless one concedes that she had arranged everything, weighed everything, in advance; that she had been preparing her deed for a long time, and had organized it down to the smallest detail, choosing the time of year and the time of day to be sure that the world would see Paul's death as nothing but an accident.

In that case, one would be rediscovering the strong-willed, dominant, organized Laure one had briefly suspected in the seemingly tender and naïve young girl who was hatching her plot to appropriate the Bernardini fortune.

And she had thought of everything. She knew that in the fashion of that day and that society, it was judged right and proper to censure a domestic scandal more severely than a crime. By exposing Paul's opprobrious conduct for all to see, Laure would have lost her own dignity, whereas her crime, if by mischance it was discovered, could only invest her with a tragic halo. Laure preferred tragedy to vaudeville, the status of criminal to that of one who was by common knowledge a deceived wife.

All this, of course, is only surmise.

People say that Paul had retired early, taking his rifle up to his bedroom to clean it.

People readily visualize him in that room, which, although rather sparsely furnished, was vast; he would have been sitting before the fireplace, where the fire was dying down and then leaping up again briefly in red and white flames. Paul would have laid out his gear nearby: the rods and the felt swabs, the oil can. By some inadvertence, he had neglected to unload the weapon; a cartridge remained in it, one of the type used to shoot wild boar. He released the trigger. He received the blast squarely in the forehead.

Laure, with smothered step, climbed the stairs, the gun under her arm. She could walk lightly, despite her weight; her foot pressed softly on each step, and she avoided places where the wood creaked. Paul had time only to raise his head above the newspaper and to open his mouth in a shout of stupefaction and terror; the gun fired; the man, head shattered, collapsed. Before the dying fire, Laure placed the open oil can, the felt swabs, the rods. Then she arranged Paul in a natural pose—a pose natural for a man who, out of absent-mindedness, has just put a bullet in his forehead.

Thérèse's bedroom was located directly above Paul's. She could not have failed to hear the shot. She must have come down, must have rushed down. Laure was holding the still warm weapon. Or else she had dropped it; surprised by the recoil of the butt, she was rubbing her bruised shoulder. She was pale, and the bitter juice of vengeance wet her mouth.

Was Thérèse afraid? Did she suppose that one bullet remained for her?

It was she, perhaps, who placed around the room the various objects destined to give credibility to the version of an accident. Laure forced her, by dint of threats, to become her accomplice. Then both women went out, closing the door behind them. The gravity of her crime struck Laure suddenly, and she began to tremble. Whereupon Thérèse supported Laure's heavy body as far as her bed. She laid her down on it. Drunk with amazement and horror, she hurled herself on Laure, and the two of them, clasping each other in a close, quivering embrace, communed in a kind of atrocious voluptuousness. After minutes of strange delirium, Thérèse went to sound the alarm.

One must take Théodore into account also. How could Théodore, who slept on the same floor as Thérèse, have let his master be struck down without saying a word?

But Théodore—as the inquest brought out—had not retired

to his cubbyhole, which he occupied only in winter, preferring to sleep in one of the outbuildings until cold weather evicted him; he had begun to raise his rabbits and was comfortable in their company.

Théodore could not have heard the shot—that is what he claimed afterward—and could have arrived only after the tragedy, summoned by Thérèse.

One can speculate, also, that Laure and Thérèse had acted in concert.

Had Laure confronted Thérèse with the choice between her friendship and her husband's life? Or, instead, was the friendship of Laure and Thérèse so strong and so exclusive that Paul was held to be an inconvenient third and had to disappear? Did Thérèse decide that Paul, having been guilty of forcing her to betray Laure, must die? Was it Thérèse, and not Laure, who pressed the trigger? (She knew how to use a gun, no doubt, from having often frequented the shooting galleries at fairs.)

It is impossible to know how Paul Bernardini died. The doctor, hastily summoned, could only verify the death and state that, on the basis of all the evidence, it was the result of an unfortunate accident.

The inquest was brief. Laure was questioned, then Thérèse, but they could not throw much light on what had happened. Paul had gone up to his room early; he intended to oil his gun after a beat that had lasted all day. His wife and his servant, sleeping in their respective rooms, had been awakened by a shot. They had come on the run, only to discover the tragedy.

Laure did not weep. Upright and imposing, she responded curtly to the coroner's questions, as if her husband's death did not concern her. It was this unfeeling attitude that made some people suspect her.

They were not believed.

The notion that Paul Bernardini could have committed suicide was not believed either. Why would he have done so?

The children were called home for the funeral. They appeared a little dazed, almost indifferent. Laure concealed a face of marble under a large black veil. Thérèse kept her eyes lowered. Théo cried.

In church, Mme. Laure stared steadily at the capital of a column. As happens in the decoration of Gothic chapels, among the sacred images, the virgins and the blessed, the figure of a grimacing horned devil had been sculpted; captured in stone, it was, perhaps, the symbol of the evil thoughts enshrined in the depths of an austere heart. Mme. Laure Bernardini could not tear her eyes from it. The De Profundis reverberated around her; the widow, her veil thrown back, contemplated the demon.

The service continued with the interment of Paul in the family vault. Monumental, surmounted by a heavy stone cross, it was secured by a black-barred grille.

At the end of the ceremony, Laure put the key to the grille in her handbag.

Mme. Laure holds the cage open while Mme. Thérèse reaches cautiously inside. The big rabbit has sought refuge against the far side; she is shaking with fear.

Mme. Thérèse tells the creature to be still; what a fine thing it would be if it were to bite her.

Mme. Laure counsels prudence; she knows only too well that the animal is dangerous.

Mme. Thérèse has seized the long ears; triumphantly, she laughs a little senile laugh, a meager cascade over a bed of stones.

It is dark, but Mme. Laure is holding a flashlight, and in the beam of light the eyes of the rabbit glisten, translucent like jelly. Mme. Thérèse gives a tug. The animal resists, but gives in little by little; they hear the nails of her paws scratch and tear, struggling vainly to grip the ground. The rabbit is hauled from the

132

cage. She is fat and heavy; she wriggles convulsively, flattens herself, draws herself up, kicks with her back feet; she is mad with fear.

Mme. Thérèse says that the animal is defending itself too well, that she is going to have to let go. Mme. Laure opens the burlap bag and imprisons the rabbit in it. Mme. Thérèse ties the moving bundle, and together they carry it toward the house.

The kitchen light is on. Mme. Thérèse lays her burden on the table and rubs her hands, complaining that they hurt. Mme. Laure holds the bag down firmly, for it threatens momentarily to jump to the ground.

Mme. Thérèse turns to the table, opens the drawer, and takes out the knife.

It is an old kitchen knife. It has been sharpened so often that its blade has been worn thin; instead of running straight from handle to tip, the blade sinuates and curves at several places. The tip is pointed. The handle is black.

Mme. Laure asks if Thérèse is going to strike blindly.

Mme. Thérèse says that she is going to partly open the bag and get hold of the ears.

Mme. Laure shivers; she says that she should have fetched her shawl.

Mme. Thérèse replies that there is no time for that now.

Through the widened top of the bag, the head of the rabbit appears. Mme. Thérèse tightens the burlap around its neck.

Mme. Laure says that they are getting nowhere, and Mme. Thérèse asks harshly if she wishes to take her place.

Mme. Laure sits down heavily in a rush-bottomed chair; she tells Mme. Thérèse to lay the bag in her lap.

Mme. Thérèse is holding the animal by the ears; the bag in which its body is contained is wedged between Mme. Laure's thighs.

Mme. Thérèse pulls on the ears with her left hand to expose the throat. With her right hand, she raises the knife.

Mme. Laure asks if they could not suspend the unfolding of

133

the action a moment; the animal's nails are digging into her thighs through the bag and her skirt.

Mme. Thérèse says that they must hurry.

Mme. Laure sighs; happily, she says, rabbits do not scream.

Mme. Thérèse says that sometimes they do scream, and Mme. Laure turns a little paler.

Mme. Thérèse asks if Mme. Laure is ready, and then she plunges in the knife.

The big rabbit makes a squeak. Mme. Laure is trembling. Mme. Thérèse twists the knife in the wound and the blood spurts out and flows, thick, red, dark, into the bowl that wobbles in Mme. Laure's hands.

Mme. Thérèse explains that she has seen rabbits killed in a variety of ways: one can tear out an eye, or break the neck, or throw them against a wall. As for herself, she knows only the knife method.

The animal's body inside the bag has become limp.

Mme. Laure and Mme. Thérèse carry the dead rabbit out into the garden; they lay it in the cage; they only half close the gate to the hutch.

They proceed to throw away the stained bag; they empty the contents of the bowl down the drain in the sink.

Mme. Laure says that she dreads the shouts of Théodore when he finds his rabbit with her throat cut.

Mme. Thérèse laughs. Théodore will think that his rabbit was bled by a weasel.

Mme. Laure is staggering; she says that she is ready to drop with sleep.

The old women have regained their bedrooms.

The garden is only a dark tangle of intertwining growth against which the white posts on the balustrade stand out like a row of upturned vases. Moonlight softens the colors of the flagstones on the long, narrow terrace; it resembles a huge tomb strewn with flowers.